The Bartender

A THRILLER

LEAH ORR

This book is printed in the USA.

The Bartender. Copyright © 2022 by Leah Orr.
All rights reserved.

The Library of Congress Cataloging-in-Publication Data is available upon request.

First Edition: February 2022
ISBN 979-8-9855783-1-7 paperback
ISBN 979-8-9855783-2-4 hardcover

Leah Orr
Jensen Beach, Florida

In a book club? Want signed copies?
You can contact Leah directly at:
www.leahorr.com
or by email:
orrplace1@bellsouth.net

Dedicated to my husband, Wayne Orr, everyone's favorite bartender at The Dirty Orr (our home pub)— well-known for his generous hospitality, bar tricks, unique cocktail recipes, and terrible dad jokes.

The Bartender

Leah Orr

Keeper of secrets, shaken or stirred, but always devoured.
                              —The Bartender

Prologue

S he raised her martini glass—a customary gesture to the ladies, bartender, and patrons.

"Cheers," she said, while hoisting her key lime martini to the assembled crowd. The key lime martini was one of the most celebrated signature specialty drinks at the Flamingo Lounge Speakeasy, secretly hidden behind the old jukebox in the lobby bar at the Opulence Resort & Spa.

The bartender assembled with perfection: 4 ounces of vanilla vodka, 3 tablespoons of condensed milk, and 3.5 tablespoons of both lime and pineapple juice. The bartender then shook and strained the concoction into a crystal Mikasa martini glass and centered it gingerly upon a square purple cocktail napkin with a generous smile. A photoworthy masterpiece. The cocktail, creamy both in color and texture, gave off a tart scent of effervescent citrus comparable to key lime pie. A graham cracker crust along the rim was held perfectly in place by corn syrup and garnished with a key lime wheel and just a touch of whipped cream for prosperity.

She took a small sip, licked her lips, and declared to her captive audience, "Vengeance never tasted so sweet." She then took two large gulps and, with her tongue, finished off the graham cracker rim and smiled a wide, indulgent grin.

Thirty seconds later, she slumped slightly over the bar, holding her midsection, then suddenly fainted, falling sideways off the barstool. She thrashed around on the floor, mouth foaming with lime green bubbling saliva. Her fingers curled, blood trickled from her nose and ears, and her right foot shook uncontrollably, releasing her loose-laced red plaid Jeffrey Campbell high-heeled boot from her writhing body.

The bar patrons watched transfixed, but did not budge to help her in any way. Instead, the ladies formed a circle around her while exhibiting no immediate signs of shock. Faces expressionless, the horror mirrored in each other's eyes eventually gave in to twisted smiles and an eerie sense of glee as it became obvious that her revenge was short-lived.

After approximately three silent minutes, the woman stopped all movement as her eyelids slowly crept open. Still, no one spoke a word. The ladies and bar patrons just leered maliciously at the woman's lifeless body on the cold marble floor.

The bartender waited approximately fifteen minutes before making the obligatory call to both hotel security and 911.

Four Months Earlier . . .

Chapter One

Selena

A fortune-teller tarot card reader at Universal Studios Orlando once told me that my career as a police officer would end abruptly and that it was imperative to learn how to control my anger, because it would not suit me well and may very well destroy me. I should have heeded that advice.

That fateful day, my alarm rang at 4:45 a.m. just like every other morning. The day started off well. A cup of french vanilla coffee, a beautiful sunrise to enjoy from the lanai, and I watched in fascination the cardinals fight squirrels for food from the feeder. By the time I got to the precinct, the clerk admitted that the evening shift was slow and suggested that since not much was going on in Palm Beach this week, things around here should be quiet. Quiet it was until 2:00 p.m., shortly before my shift was about to end, when my partner and I caught a call about a domestic violence disturbance.

As we pulled into the driveway of 986 River Edge Dr., I heard a woman scream and glass shatter before even getting out of the squad car. With my hand on my gun, still holstered, I knocked loudly on the door three times, then cried out, "Police! Open the door!"

A large, bald man pushed the door open boldly, filling out the doorway almost entirely with his expansive height and width. His body was painted with tattoos. A large skull on his neck stared back, taunting me. A small painted teardrop rested underneath his left eye, proudly depicting a life he stole—a gangster's medal of honor.

"Step aside," I demanded. I wanted to take a closer look at the woman who was suffering from the opposite end of his fist.

"No," he said adamantly, challenging my authority.

"Back down, and show me your hands," said my partner, Jake, while standing within inches of his face. "Step away, and allow my partner the ability to talk to your girlfriend in private."

The young girl, tiny in stature, could not have been any taller than four feet eleven. She sat looking desperately sad, hunched over, cradling her stomach with both arms, rocking back and forth on the ratty couch within the dilapidated apartment. She was layered in bruises, colored blue, black, and purple, the freshest bruises bright pink, and blood streaming slowly from her nose. I took a handkerchief from my pocket, an important tool of my trade, and gave it to her to wipe her delicate face. A beautiful jade pendant necklace hung low between her tiny breasts. The green gem sparkled brilliantly in defiance against her battered body in this broken place.

"That is a beautiful necklace," I said.

"A gift from my mom, 'a jade for my beautiful Jade.' That is what my mom said when she gave it to me." As she recalled that touching memory on her sixteenth birthday, fresh tears filled her beautiful green eyes. Tears cascaded down her cheeks as her chest hollowed, heaved, and released her anguish. I could instantly feel the love she felt for her mom and the intensity of the pain inflicted upon her today all at once as a flood of emotion overwhelmed me. I hugged her in that moment. Not protocol, but I could not resist.

"Call your mom," I insisted.

"I will," she promised.

After the confrontation with the boyfriend and chatting with Jade, I took photos of her battered body and the disarray of the apartment. Jake collected their identification, wrote the report, and suggested we talk to the neighbors. She stated, however, that she was unwilling to press charges and that somehow this was all her fault and we should leave before we get her into any more trouble. Jake said, "Well, if she is not willing to press charges, there is nothing more we can do to help here. Let's go, Selena."

"Okay," I said reluctantly. Turning to the bald man, I added, "But if you touch her again and I get called back here, you will regret it, and I mean that." I handed Jade my business card and pleaded with her to call me any time, day or night. "If you ever need my assistance, I will always be here for you. I promise."

"Give me your phone," she said.

"Okay," I agreed. Again, not protocol, but I felt compelled to keep in touch with this girl who so obviously needed a friend to reach out to and rely upon.

She took the phone from my hand, typed her name and number into my contacts, and said, "Please keep in touch."

The anger on her boyfriend's face was palpable as she put her number in my phone.

Just as we were walking out the door, through my peripheral vision, I saw him strike her square in the nose. Without flinching, I rushed back inside, punched him hard, and heard the delightful sound of his jaw crack like a walnut smashing, giving in to the force of a powerful nutcracker. He fell sideways at just the perfect angle, allowing his temple to meet the corner edge of the glass coffee table. It wasn't my punch or the broken jaw that ultimately killed him but rather the geometry of the fall.

And just like that, my eight-year career as a police officer was over.

Chapter Two

Her

T he contract was hardly dry from Leslie's signature when she suggested that she and Zander, her current ally and companion, visit the new property. This was Leslie's first hotel acquisition. She owned many other properties that included apartment buildings in New York City, malls in Miami and Orlando, and a small winery in Sonoma, but this was her first hotel, and never had she been so excited. The Opulence Resort & Spa was quite an acquisition. An exquisite five-star hotel, exclusive and perfectly nestled in the heart of Florida's beautiful Palm Beach, it was most known for its spectacular sunrises and notorious for its world-famous and infamous guests over the span of the past hundred years.

The hotel was worth north of three hundred million dollars. The waterfront property it sat upon was worth many millions more. Her stake in the property was only a small share, but she would become the managing partner, as the other owners preferred their ownership to remain silent.

The price tag of forty million dollars would have been a pipe dream for most investors, but for Leslie that was chump change. She had what some people call "stupid money." You know, those people who have so much money they simply could not spend it all in a lifetime or two, or even ten.

Leslie was not born into money but rather begged, borrowed, stole, and slept her way to fortune. With no real family of her own after her parents' car accident just shy of her fifteenth birthday, she and her brother were forced to live apart in different homes within the foster care system. By age sixteen, Leslie filled out rather nicely. She stood five feet eleven inches tall, her body voluptuous in an Anna Nicole Smith kind of way, without the blonde hair but rather ebony curls. Her foster mom used to refer to her hair as "the ebony waves of wonder." Her biological mom, a Jamaican Islander, and her father, Australian, allowed for the perfect mixture of their ancestors' best genes, conspiring together to create the fabric of her gorgeous hair with a perfect mix of curl, thickness, and texture, similar to wigs worn by Beyonce or J.Lo when performing on stage.

She was content with her new family and high school but detested being poor, not so much because she needed money for food or entertainment but because she dreamed about one day having a wardrobe full of designer shoes, dresses, and jewelry. Leslie loved fashion and the mental and emotional power she felt in new designer fabrics, a self-confidence that immediately radiated as soon as she was fully dressed, when the fabric of the clothing touched the fabric of her soul. She often reminded herself of the beautiful clothing she once wore when her parents were alive as she stared down upon her dirty Converse sneakers and jeans that were two sizes too large for her figure, barely held up by one of her foster brother's belts.

That would all change, however, when she met Harry Rothlesberg. Harry was a little-known, self-made millionaire who made his fortune in mens socks, of all things ridiculous, she often mused. His most popular socks were his wool blend, moisture-wicking boot socks designed for US Army troops during the war in Vietnam. He cared for her deeply and the way she made him feel special, like he was the only man on earth for her. Often she was reminded of a little tidbit of advice her mother once gave her: People don't fall in love with people. People fall in love with how other people make them feel about themselves.

Harry was in love, and he didn't let a little thing like seventy years between them keep them from getting married on her eighteenth birthday. He called her his "cuddle bug" and enjoyed her beauty and doting attention, but it was her warm, large-breasted hugs that always put a big smile on his face. She, on the other hand, painstakingly counted the days until his long overdue fatal stroke, 889 days into their marriage.

Shortly after the funeral, Leslie convinced the estate executor attorney to alter the will by listing her, and her alone, as the beneficiary to his three-hundred-million-dollar estate instead of his two bastard sons who couldn't be bothered to visit him in the hospital after any of his three strokes, let alone find the time to visit during the last few weeks of his life in hospice.

"I deserve this," she pleaded with the executor. "No one cared for him other than me. If you do this for me, I will be sure to pay your attorney fees. What would that cost be, anyway? Two million, three million dollars for your time?"

"Five million," he said. And that was how Leslie made her first 300 million dollars, or 295 million to be exact.

Chapter Three

Selena

Today when the alarm clock rang, I did not move. I laid in my bed staring up at the ceiling above me, trying to make shapes out of the cracks in the paint. I could make out a one-eared bunny, a star, and a double-scooped ice cream cone. Suddenly I felt hungry. The sun gleamed in from the window, reminding me that although I may be feeling crappy, the day was determined to move forward.

In an instant, a daunting memory filled my mind. The third grade came back to me in a flurry. The slide memory. The slide at recess was the best part about the morning break before lunchtime. It stood about ten feet tall, which, as a kid, seemed giant. The slide twisted in the middle and spit out children in the opposite direction. My best friend, Mary, and I would run to the slide as soon as the bell rang every day.

One day, the new boy in the classroom, Elmer, coaxed some of the other boys to hide under the slide, so when we slid out they would jump out at us for a scare. But it wasn't just a scare they were excited about; it was the subsequent showering of acorns they collected from the playground floor.

Mary went down the slide first, and when I heard a scream and giggling, I didn't think much of it. When I slid out of the slide, the boys jumped out and threw acorns on me as well. I was startled but became angry when I saw Mary holding her eye, crying in pain. "What did you do to her?" I said, demanding an immediate answer.

"She is just being a baby," said Elmer.

"She is crying because you hurt her eye with one of those acorns. You need to apologize and bring her to the school nurse."

"Nope," he said, then looked back at his friends, and the boys laughed at me.

"You need to apologize and take her to the nurse or you will be sorry," I said adamantly. "I mean it." Then something unexpected happened. He pulled my pony tail hard, real hard, so much so that tears escaped from my left eye. So I did what I thought any nine-year-old girl would do in that situation. I punched him in the nose— hard, real hard. Because, you see, we recently learned in science class Newton's third law of motion: For every action, there is an equal and opposite reaction. It only seemed fair.

That was the defense I went with when I had to explain this situation in Principal Stuart's office. What I wanted to say was that he was a jerk and he deserved it, but I learned at an early age that it is important to know your audience and adjust your story accordingly. That is why I relied on Sir Isaac Newton as my defense.

The icing on the cake for me was that Elmer never returned to school. I told everyone that he was sent to the glue factory. My third-grade self thought I was a comedian. Needless to say, no one dared to mess with me or my friend Mary ever again.

Growing up with a deceased father who was not around to protect us, my four sisters and I learned to stick up for ourselves at a very early age. My sisters mastered payback by the use of cunning and revenge. For me—rage and pain.

If I am being honest, it was no real surprise to me that my career would end this way. Just yesterday I had the world at my feet. Today I was plagued by only a small financial settlement and many months of required therapy ahead of me. I couldn't stay home feeling sorry for myself, so I called my sister for help. Talia is my eldest sister and always steps up whenever any of us need her, no matter how challenging the situation. I picked up my cell phone and dialed.

"Hey, Talia. How are you? Have you got any job openings at the hotel?" I asked, trying to sound as upbeat as possible in my current state of misery.

"Oh no," she said. "What did you fuck up this time, Selena?"

"What makes you say I fucked something up? Maybe I just want to do something different. Eight years of police work is enough. It's grueling, all sad stories, drug addicts, and domestic violence. I think I just need a change of scenery."

"You got fired, right?" asked Talia.

"Yeah, I did. It's a long story, but I need a job." I tried to come off optimistic, but it just came out sounding desperate.

"Sometimes, Selena, I wonder if I am going to have to take care of you for your entire life. You are almost thirty years old, still fucking up everything you touch."

I expected as much from Talia, always overly dramatic. She ranted on for a few more minutes. Blah, blah, blah, bad attitude this and bad temper that, then finally ended with, "You need to grow up and be responsible. How in the fuck did you screw up a career as a cop? Cops can literally *kill* people and *still* collect a pension."

"Um, well, apparently not anymore," I admitted shamefully.

"Don't tell me you—"

"Yes, but he deserved it—asshole, thug, gangster, girlfriend-beating bastard," I said defiantly.

"Well, as usual, I've got you, Sis," she said. "Come in tomorrow. I have a job for you at the hotel as a bartender at the speakeasy. The previous bartender left unexpectedly. I think this job will suit you well for the time being, until you can get your shit together. By the way, did you tell Mom?"

"Never. She'd beat me with a stick," I said.

"If you're lucky," said Talia.

"Thank you for the job," I said gratefully. "I can always count on you."

"Don't fuck this up. I am the general manager now," she said. "Just don't kill anyone."

Chapter Four

A Brand New Selena

My alarm rang at 4:45 a.m. because old habits die hard. Today I felt renewed, and strangely, for a moment, I was taken back to a time twenty-five years ago, when I was a little girl lying on the couch, my grandma playing a Frank Sinatra 8-track. I could clearly hear the music and Sinatra singing . . .

> *So take a deep breath, pick yourself up, dust yourself off, and start all over again.*

Thankful for the beautiful memory from a brilliant woman, I scampered out of bed feeling inspired. I got dressed and drove straight to the beauty salon. I asked the stylist to help me put my cop days behind me.

"I need a new start," I said. "Something stunning—unconventional." We settled upon an edgy cut with a violet ombre hue. At home I chose a perfect shade of lipstick, eye shadow, and bold dangle earrings to match my new professional look. This is the new me, I told myself in the bathroom mirror, and I am *not* going to fuck this up!

Chapter Five

Selena & The Caretaker

After finishing all of the required and very tedious paperwork, along with fingerprinting and a background check, I was told if all went well, I could start the following day promptly at 4:00 p.m.

"Don't be late. You will have to get the bar set up by five o'clock. Our local regular patrons often show up promptly at opening, ready to wash away their grief and indulge themselves with your charm. Get a good night's sleep and prepare to entertain and be delightful," said the lady from Human Resources with a name I would never remember. That was a strange statement, I thought. Prepare to be delightful. Hmmm.

As I was walking through the lobby to return home, I was stopped by a man named Hubert. "Hello, Selena," he said. He tipped an invisible hat toward me while he bowed gently.

"I am Hubert, the caretaker of the speakeasy. I would love to show you around and tell you a few tales about its history."

"Sure. I would love that," I said enthusiastically. "I have heard so much about this speakeasy, and I am very excited to learn more about it."

At first glance, Hubert looked like a strange fellow. An old-timer, maybe sixty-five, seventy, or even eighty years old, it was hard to tell if he was older and looked good for his age or on the younger side but had seen hard times. Hubert was very tall, pushing six feet, ten inches was my best guess. Slim, with long arms and slender feet, I wondered how he could find clothes and especially shoes that would fit his unusual physique.

"Follow me," he said insistently. As I followed him though the lobby, he told me that the hotel, as seen today, is quite different from its original design. The hotel's five hundred oceanfront suites within twenty stories, each having extended balconies to allow guests the enjoyment of beautiful sunrises from the coast, also enjoy the colorful aftermath of the sunset as it cascades over from the opposite coast. The hotel, established in 1920, was designed to accommodate nobility and wealthy Americans. It was originally an eighty-room palace in a class of its own. Just over a hundred years ago, the Flamingo Lounge was one of the more popular places to be in the Roaring Twenties. The Opulence Resort was designed with elements of European architectural and artistic influence. The hotel was modeled after some of the most magnificent villas in Rome. As many as fifty artisans were brought over by sea from all over Italy, from Milan to Rome. Together they designed and created intricate paintings displayed across the ceilings and walls of the three-hundred-foot-long main lobby and first-floor private meeting rooms.

"The lobby bar was formerly a stage for entertainers, and the speakeasy was previously a semiprivate bar for male patrons to smoke cigars, drink whisky, and conduct business in obscurity away from women and nosy guests," Hubert explained.

"Fascinating," I said. "Tell me more."

"Well, when Prohibition began and alcohol was outlawed, the hotel built a wall between the entertainment stage and the gentlemen's bar to keep out coppers and riffraff. The gentlemen's bar then became known to those invited as the Flamingo Lounge Speakeasy."

We entered the speakeasy through a staircase behind the front desk and walked through a long, dark tunnel illuminated by ambient light a foot in front of us, welcoming us with every step.

"Come on now, missy. Don't fiddle-fart," he said as we ambled along. When we reached the entrance, he took an antique key out of his front pocket and unlocked an ancient stone door. "This is an alternative entrance to the bar so that you do not have to mix with the patrons on your way in or out. There is an identical stone door on the opposite end for certain invited guests who demand anonymity."

"Okay," I said. "Is it important to stay clear of the patrons? Should I be worried about the regulars?"

"You should always be prepared for a quick escape in unusual circumstances that you could not imagine at this moment. It is best to be prepared at all times. As a former police officer, I am sure you understand the need to protect yourself and fully grasp all means of egress if a need arises and you are compelled to use them. The speakeasy is windowless, for obvious reasons, as it is a secret refuge for Palm Beach's most prominent and our patrons' private party guests."

"Understood," I said.

Walking into the speakeasy, I was in awe of such an exquisite site. *Wow* was the only word that filled my brain at the moment in big, bold letters: W-O-W! The hairs stood up on my arms and neck as I took in the spectacle of the bar's extravagance and intrigue.

Soft jazz music played from Bose surround sound speakers. An unusual aroma that was hard to describe filled my senses. The bar smelled like cherry vanilla mixed with clean linen. The room was not cold but crisp, and I guessed the hotel must pump in oxygen the same way hotels in Las Vegas do to keep patrons high-spirited. Lively guests tend to stay longer and drink more.

A large circular bar that could seat thirty people comfortably was centered within the room. The bar top was highlighted by purple under-counter lighting. Dangling brilliantly above the bar was a ten-foot-wide chandelier hovering in celebration, with a thousand tiny purple incandescent light bulbs. Two layers of illuminated shelves were centered within the bar. There were bottles of liquor, all shapes and sizes, most of which were unfamiliar to me—brands I'd never heard of that must have been popular in the Roaring Twenties and days of Prohibition.

Against the back wall, a six-foot neon flamingo, with its pink feathers flickering on and off atop its head, added even more charm to this lifelike, iconic Florida bird, the speakeasy's namesake.

"This place is spectacular," I said in awe.

"Yes it is, my dear," Hubert agreed. "Your personal key has been laid out for you on the counter; please take care of this place and its patrons. I am counting on you to treat this place and its people like friends and family, as you would in your own home."

"I most certainly will," I said. I walked behind the bar and looked around, taking it all in, and immediately felt like taking this job was going to be one of the best decisions I had made in a very long time. I felt like this place was just sitting here waiting for me.

After a few minutes of investigating my new work space, I took out my cell phone and snapped photos of the unusual liquor varieties in antique bottles and the speakeasy's specialty drink recipes within a very old leather-bound bartender's bible. If this book could talk, I thought, it must have fascinating and delicious tales of America's past, during both grand and tumultuous times.

My intention was to spend the evening on the internet absorbing copious amounts of information about this strange alcohol and some of the Flamingo Lounge's signature drinks to better prepare myself for my first day on the job. When I turned toward Hubert to thank him for the tour, he was already gone.

Chapter Six

Her

When Leslie's Bentley stretch limousine pulled up under the hotel's porte-cochère, she was enamored by the hotel's beauty even before getting out of the limo. The hotel's grand entrance, which could be enjoyed before entering the lobby, had floor-to-ceiling windows displaying enormous chandeliers, gold drapes, and designer marble floors.

Three valet attendants aligned and greeted the limo upon Leslie and Zander's arrival. The driver lowered the window, and the valet said, "Welcome to the Opulence Resort and Spa. Will you be staying with us this evening?"

"Ms. Lewis will be staying here now and every evening, sir," said Oscar, her driver. "She is the new owner."

Oscar pulled over, stepped out, opened Leslie's car door, and said, "Enjoy your day, ma'am. Text me when you require my services once more."

"Thank you, Oscar," she said. "Don't go too far, just in case I need you later this evening."

"Yes, ma'am," he said, then opened Zander's door for him. "Good luck, sir," he said. Good luck—yes, I am definitely going to need that, Zander thought. More than you know. This is going to be a very difficult day.

"I need a drink," said Zander.

"My thought exactly," said Leslie. "First thing I want to do is check out that speakeasy. I've heard so much about it," she said enthusiastically.

The power couple walked through the revolving entrance door and into the lobby, where the aroma of lavender and vanilla enticed the senses. They were greeted by two bellmen and the concierge director. All three stood stoically, like toy soldiers, and nodded their heads in unison as Leslie and Zander entered. One of the bellmen said, "Welcome to the Opulence Resort and Spa. Enjoy your stay here with us. The front desk is located to your right, and the lobby bar is straight ahead. Please, may I help you with your luggage?"

"No, thank you, but tell me, where can I find the speakeasy?" Leslie asked with anticipation.

"I am not sure what you mean," said the bellman.

In a quick effort to change the subject, the concierge director offered, "I would be delighted to help you with dinner arrangements or entertainment preferences while staying with us. Here is my business card. Please call me directly for all of your personal needs."

Leslie angrily snatched the business card from his hand. She stared a few moments too long into each of their eyes to see if any of them would flinch or inadvertently give off any telling insight into the location of the speakeasy. Maybe one of them would look away toward its direction. Leslie had no such luck. Hmm, the speakeasy really is a secret, she thought.

Leslie then made a phone call to the real estate attorney, who responded with the information she requested. Leslie and Zander walked through the lobby into the lobby bar and continued toward the back wall. There, against the wall, stood a 1950s-style Wurlitzer jukebox. She took a quarter from her Chanel purse, pushed it through the coin slot, and pressed the letter *B* and the number *2*. After a noisy clicking sound, an old, warped 45 fell upon the turntable. A rusty metal arm pulled away from its resting spot and played "Let's Misbehave" by Irving Aaronson, which was popular in 1928.

> *We're all alone, no chaperone*
> *Can get our number*
> *The world's in slumber*
> *Let's misbehave*

At approximately fifteen seconds into the song, a beeping sound came from behind the red velvet curtain draped behind the jukebox. Leslie and Zander parted the red curtain and found themselves in a dark and drafty hallway. A dusty floodlight greeted them from above, and a small stone door was illuminated. The door, a throwback from the Dark Ages, looked like an old prison door from a European castle. The doorbell to the left of the door was lit up, blinking red, and a motion sensor camera above moved slowly toward their faces.

"Hello," said Selena, the voice coming from above their heads from a speaker they could not detect. "Welcome to the Flamingo Lounge." Then the voice articulated very slowly, "My name is Selena. Tell me your secrets," the husky, sexy, and mysterious voice coming from what seemed like oblivion.

"Hmm, a secret? Well, you will be one of the first to know that I am the new owner here, and I would love to meet you," Leslie said.

"I would be delighted," said the mysterious voice. "Please press the blinking doorbell and come on in." Leslie pressed the doorbell, the bell blinked green, and the stone door slid open clamoring to the left across the hallway floor, traveling noisily along a metal track, leaving a small two-and-a-half-foot opening with just enough room to carefully slither through to a dark and chilly tunnel. There they were welcomed by plate-sized purple circular emergency lights along the center of the floor's path that would lead them straight into the speakeasy.

"Well, this is going to be quite fun," suggested Leslie.

"If you say so," said Zander sarcastically. "Our destiny awaits."

Chapter Seven

Selena

H ere we go," I said out loud. A new
me, with a new career, in a new
place. I had a quick reflection about
words of advice from the Human Resources
director yesterday: "Be delightful." Those
words reverberated in my mind for the few
moments it took for Leslie and Zander to
enter the speakeasy.

Chapter Eight

Her

It was just past 5:00 p.m. when Leslie and Zander sauntered in like royalty. The bar was empty and there stood Selena, carefully removing water stains from martini glasses with a purple chenille cloth.

"Hello and welcome," said Selena. "Tell me your poison, and I'll relieve your troubles."

"I will have a glass of your finest Bordeaux, and Zander will have a dirty martini. Extra dirty, please. He likes his martinis like he likes his women."

Selena giggled nervously. "My pleasure. You are my first patrons. I am new here, and as luck would have it, my first customers are the new owners. I hope these cocktails will not disappoint." Selena poured a glass of Bordeaux Chateau Canon vintage 2009 for Leslie and crafted a dirty martini, old school, like the old bartender's bible suggested. The martini was concocted with 2.5 ounces of Old London Dock gin, .5 ounces of dry Martini & Rossi vermouth, and two dashes of Regan's orange bitters. She added a splash of olive juice to make it extra dirty. Selena stirred the cocktail slowly with plenty of ice, then strained and poured it into a chilled martini glass, and finally garnished it with a classic green olive skewered with a toothpick in the shape of a flamingo.

"I enjoyed the adventurous entrance into the lounge. It was very exciting. 'Tell me your secrets' was a nice touch," Leslie said.

"I love secrets, and you would be surprised what people would tell a stranger in the dark, and more so in precarious situations. As a former police officer, I have eight years' experience in finding interesting ways to get people to tell me the most intimate details about their lives, some of which no one else knows, and other details people would not even admit to themselves," said Selena while admiring the beautiful new owner. Selena was mostly impressed by Leslie's confidence and the allure of her large brown eyes that seemed as though they could lure you into an abyss if she chose to lead you there. She made a mental note to beware of this woman. She did not seem the type to be reckoned with.

Changing the subject, Selena transferred her attention to Zander. "Zander, that is an unusual name. You're not the Zander that worked with my sister Talia are you?"

"Why yes, he is," Leslie answered for him. Selena looked at Leslie, then Zander, wondering if this woman always answered for him and how Zander felt about that. Does he like a dominant woman? Does he cower in fear of what she might do should he step out of line? I couldn't really tell yet.

"Does Talia know you are here? She is the general manager now," Selena said.

"Yes, I heard that and no, not yet. We just arrived. I will be sure to drop by the office soon," said Zander nervously.

"I am not sure she will be happy to see you after what transpired in New York between the two of you, but I truly wish you luck. I can't pretend to know all of the details, but whatever you did to anger her, please just start off with a sincere apology. That is my best advice."

"Well," Leslie said, before indulging in her forty-five-dollar glass of Bordeaux, "upon entrance, I told *you* my secret. It seems as though you may already know Zander's, so now it's *your* turn to tell me yours."

"Let's just say I am so happy to be here and that I killed to get this job."

"Well, well, Selena, I can already tell that you and I are going to be friends," said Leslie with a genuine smile.

Chapter Nine

Selena

It wasn't long after Leslie and Zander left the speakeasy when an old man stumbled into the entrance, already looking tipsy. The old man was no taller than five feet, hunched over, walking toward me with a cane. He had a large gray mustache, beard, and wild and wiry hair. The spitting image of Einstein, I thought. "Hello," I said. "Welcome to the Flamingo Lounge. How did you get in here?" I thought I would have to allow patrons to enter by buzzing them in through the doorbell.

The old man said, "Hello, pretty lady. So you are the new girl. I heard a lot about you. Each regular patron plays their own particular song on the jukebox, the jukebox recognizes us, and the stone door opens without a fuss."

"I was unaware of that. Thank you. May I ask your name?"

"I am Willy," he said while scratching his beard and fiddling with his mustache—a

45

nervous habit maybe. "Most people refer to me as old man Wilcox, but I prefer being called Willy."

"Well, hello, Willy. Tell me your poison, and I'll be happy to serve you."

"I would love a bourbon on the rocks, splash of water, please. Make sure it's Buffalo Trace. It is up there behind you on the second shelf."

"They sure do have quite an eclectic assortment of alcohol here," I said.

"Yes, they do. Buffalo Trace, for example, has been making bourbon for over two hundred years, and the distillery remained open even during Prohibition for 'medicinal purposes.' The lounge is full of hard-to-find alcohol popular in the early 1900s. Make sure to check the bartender's bible for recipes because many of your regular customers come here precisely for the specialty cocktails."

After preparing Willy's drink, I asked, "Is this your first cocktail this evening or have you already been drinking?"

"I may have had a few cocktails at the strip club down the street," he said with a wink.

"The strip club, huh?"

"Yes, but I am not going there anymore," he said.

"Okay, well, why is that?" I asked.

"One of the strippers put her balls on my chin, and I'm pretty sure that's an OSHA violation." Then Willy broke out into a big belly laugh followed by a short snort.

I could already tell that I was really going to like this old man. "Alright, Willy, can I impress you with a little bar trick?" I asked playfully.

"Well, if I enjoy your little trick, can I tell you a dirty joke?" asked Willy, tilting his head while lifting only one eyebrow. This old man Wilcox was an unusual one, alright.

I nodded and said, "Sure."

I retrieved two white napkins from the counter and placed the napkins in front of him. I took a nickel out of my pocket and placed it in the center of the napkin to his right. I then took a highball glass and placed it on top of the napkin to his left.

"Okay, Willy," I said. "I am going to make that nickel disappear."

"Go for it," he said.

I placed the highball glass over the nickel and said, "Voilà," and it disappeared. Then I said, "Now I will make it reappear."

"Okay."

47

I placed a black dinner napkin over the glass, then said, "Bibbidi bobbidi boo." I lifted the napkin from the top, along with the glass, and the nickel had returned to its original resting place.

"Very good," said Willy. "Now it's my turn."

"Go for it," I said with anticipation.

"What do you call a virgin lying on a water bed?"

"I don't know—what?"

"A cherry float!"

"Excellent," I said, laughing out loud. "Dirty bar humor. Very funny. I love it!"

At 6:00 p.m. a giant, beefy man who must've weighed over three hundred pounds traipsed into the speakeasy.

"Hello," I said. "Welcome to the Flamingo Lounge." But before I could say anything else, Willy stopped me and said, "That's Salami. He's the bouncer here. He works on the weekends and special parties and events. He can't hear you. He's wearing his headphones. He says he is learning Italian because he plans to visit Sicily soon."

"Salami?"

"Yes, actually Derek Salamoni, but everyone calls him 'The Salami' because, well, look at him!"

I laughed a little at the vision of him trying to squeeze through the tiny opening of the stone door entrance. Salami grabbed a barstool and sat by the bookcase in the back right corner of the lounge without making any eye contact with either of us.

I tried to catch his attention by waving my hands above my head. "Hellooo!" I yelled out. Salami took his earbuds out of his ears and ambled slowly over to the bar.

"Hi. I am Selena. I just wanted to introduce myself. I am new here."

"Hello, Selena. I am here to protect you and the lounge customers. I will sit in the back by the exit."

"What exit?"

"Behind the bookcase is a stone door and hallway that leads to the parking lot. Some of the customers come in or out this way instead of the lobby bar for discretionary reasons," explained Salami.

"Holy crap. How many ways are there in and out of this place," I said, but then I remembered Hubert, the caretaker, telling me about the other stone door at the opposing side of the lounge.

"Many," he said. "During Prohibition, bootleggers had one way in and out, which was through secret hallways; patrons by the jukebox; and the colored entertainers came in by the bookcase from the back parking lot. That is where I am stationed on busy nights and when we have private parties. Tonight we have a group of fifteen or twenty bankers arriving for a private gathering. They will not sit at the bar but rather occupy the couches and chat about all the ways in which they can steal more money from the rest of us, like increasing interest rates and going after big corporate clients so they can charge exorbitant fees. Disgusting group of men actually. You don't really need to look after them much. Just bring over a bunch of Yuengling beer and leave it on the coffee table. They don't make much of a fuss. Just make sure they have lots of beer."

"This place gets more interesting by the minute," I said.

Around 7:00 p.m. a lovely woman in her forties entered the speakeasy. She was dressed in a conservative Calvin Klein business suit and sensible heels. She said, "Hello, Willy, and you must be Selena, Talia's sister. She told us you were going to be our new liquid therapist."

"That's me," I said.

"I am Renata, Renata Ray, defense attorney. I am the person you call when no one else will take your case. If you've got the money, I will put in the time to make sure you don't have to pay for your crime."

"Very clever tagline," I said. "How can I help you to unleash your inner beast today?"

"Make me a Mary Pickford, would you, please? Check with the bartender's bible. I am sure you've never heard of it, but it's fabulous. Mary Pickford was a 1920s film actress. She was very popular, in case you were wondering where the drink's name came from."

"I will have to google her name when I get home later this evening," I said.

In a cocktail shaker with ice, I added 1.5 ounces of Bacardi Superior rum, 1.5 ounces of pineapple juice, 1 teaspoon of grenadine, and 5 drops of maraschino liqueur. After shaking five times, I strained it into a martini glass and garnished it with a maraschino cherry. "Wow, what a cocktail," I said, impressed with its beautiful pinkish hue.

"Bacardi Superior rum was popular in the 1930s, and not many bottles remain. Use it sparingly. It's my favorite," said Renata. She then took out a snack-sized Ziploc bag full of miniature Swedish Fish.

"Swedish Fish?" I asked. "Those were my favorite when I was a kid."

"Yes. It pairs nicely with my cocktail and a hard day's work."

"Interesting," I said. "I will have to try that sometime." Something about Renata seemed vaguely familiar to me, so I had to ask, "If you don't mind, may I ask why it is that you seem so familiar to me? Could I have seen you on TV recently?"

"Uh oh," said Willy. "The cat is out of the bag, Renata. You are famous now for all the wrong reasons."

"Yes, Selena, you may have seen me on television recently. I was the defense attorney for the man who murdered his two children. I probably should not be talking to you about this, but here it goes . . . He asked for my help, and initially I was not inclined to take the case, but he pleaded with me and promised me he didn't do it, so I agreed to take the case. After reading through all of the police reports and watching the body cam footage, it became apparent that their warrantless searches of his home and car produced evidence deemed circumstantial at best. He had no prior arrests, no previous run-ins with police, not even a traffic violation. He also had a seemingly legitimate alibi. Because of all these exculpatory factors, I was able to get him released on his own recognizance at the bond hearing."

Renata took a deep breath and a moment to collect her thoughts, and a tiny tear was shed that moistened her cheek. She wiped away the teardrop, and bravely she continued. "The evening after his release, he showed up at his ex-wife's house and murdered her along with their youngest child. The police found him sitting on the floor in a pool of blood, smiling. I can't seem to get that image out of my mind."

"I heard about that case. This was not your fault. There was no way you could have known he was such a monster, and it's your job as a criminal defense attorney to fight for his innocence and release. That is how the system works," I said empathetically, trying to calm her down, offer my condolences, and do my best not to pass judgement. "If it wasn't you that got him released, it would have been another attorney. If he was determined to kill his family, nothing would have stopped him. There was nothing you could have done."

"The thing is, my gut told me not to take this case. As a defense attorney in private practice, I can pick and choose my cases. Most of the cases I take are by gut instinct, and I should have gone with my gut," she said. "For that, I will always have regret."

"Renata, as a former police officer, I can tell you that I went with my gut in a case, hit a man, and he died. I lost my job, and I may have lost my pension. Now I am here as a reminder to you that your gut is not always the best body part to listen to in all cases," I said assuringly.

"Thank you for that," said Renata, "and also, I am sorry for your loss."

Chapter Ten

Zander and Her

As Zander walked into Talia's office, he was reminded of a quote he'd read from Lynn Johnston, a Canadian cartoonist, from her strip *For Better or For Worse*. It went something like: "A sincere apology is the superglue of life. It can repair just about anything." Well, Lynn Johnston never met Talia.

Zander opened the oversized ebony doors of the general manager's office and asked the executive secretary whether Talia was in her office at this time, and if in fact she was, could he speak with her?

"Yes, as a matter of fact she *is* in. Who may I say is requesting to speak with her?"

"I would rather not say who I am, in fear that she may not want to speak with me," said Zander. Just then, the French doors opened behind the secretary, and Talia stepped out.

"What the fuck are you doing here? Get the fuck out before I call security!" she yelled, her face flushed, lifting her pointer finger toward the door. The secretary picked up the phone and frantically began dialing.

"Talia, please, can I have a word with you? I beg of you—just hear me out," he said. "Please."

"Okay," said Talia. "Hang up the phone, Anna. I am going to speak with him in my office, with my door open. If you hear any nonsense, call hotel security."

"Yes, ma'am," said Anna, giving Zander a look that clearly meant, Don't push your luck—I'm watching you.

Zander sat down, hands shaking. Talia sat behind her desk, stared back at him, and said, "Speak."

"Okay, I'd like to start by saying that I am sincerely and wholeheartedly sorry."

"The fuck you are," said Talia.

"Please let me just tell my side of the story. Please just listen for two minutes. Then if you want me to leave, I will, and you will never see or hear from me again. Agreed?"

"Agreed."

"When I was general manager at the New York Towers Hotel in Manhattan, I was really attracted to you. I knew the hotel protocols, and I knew that upper management was not allowed to date middle management. A general manager should not be dating a catering manager due to the power dynamic. I knew this. But when you agreed to go on a date with me, I was very excited. After two dates, I thought we really had a connection."

"Fuck you!"

"You promised to listen."

"Okay, go on."

"When word got out we were dating, two friends of mine, or should I say two men I believed to be friends at the time, told me they heard you liked it rough."

"What?"

"I know, I know, let me finish."

"Jerry, my assistant GM at the time, said he knew your ex-boyfriend and that he said you liked rough sex. That stuck in my head, and I started reading about it. At the time, the book *Fifty Shades of Grey* was popular. I read the book, and in my mind I had a great idea that I thought you would enjoy."

"So you thought wrapping your Frosty the Snowman tie around my neck after the Christmas party was a good idea and that I would enjoy being strangled nearly to death while my boss hiked up my skirt in his suite. What the fuck is wrong with you? I thought you were going to rape and kill me."

"You ran out the door without letting me explain, you didn't pick up your phone, and I couldn't find you anywhere. You were not at your apartment or at work the next day. The next thing I knew, I was in Human Resources explaining what happened. The following week I was sent off to manage a property in Hawaii, and I heard you were sent here as food and beverage director at the time."

"That's right. Only word got around that I claimed you raped me and got promoted because of it. Needless to say, I had to work really hard on my reputation to prove that I didn't sleep my way into my job, or worse, make up a story in order to get promoted. So fuck you very much!"

"Maybe we could get together for a drink sometime this week and further discuss my bad behavior."

"What is it about 'fuck you' that you do not understand?"

"I am sorry, and I would like to be friends . . . or maybe more than friends," he said hopefully.

"What? No! Never! And aren't you married? Please just stay away from me."

Abruptly, Leslie walked though the door. "I see you two have worked out your differences," she said, almost giddy.

"Who the fuck are you?"

"Well, I am your new boss, owner, and managing partner of this establishment, and I do not take kindly to being spoken to in that manner. Because I like your sister Selena, I am going to let you continue to work here, but we are all going to get along nicely," she said as she lifted her finger, moving it in a circular motion to include all of them. "Is that clear?"

"Yes, ma'am," Talia said. What a fucking day!

Chapter Eleven

Selena

I often lie awake at night and wonder about some of the poor souls I encountered on the police force. I often come back around to Jade, that poor little girl, beaten and bruised. I worry and hope she is okay. I hope she called her mom that night and that she is making better choices about the kind of men she dates. Sometimes I pick up my phone to call or text her. But that wouldn't be the right thing to do. I am not a police officer anymore. She said she wanted to keep in touch, but she said that before I killed her boyfriend. A phone call would not be appropriate. I can't call her officially any longer, and we are not friends. But I truly hope she is doing well.

At 4:45 the alarm beckons and reminds me that even I deserve a new start. These days I begin my mornings with a long run before the rest of the world awakens. At dawn, I feel centered and serene and believe that all things are possible. Southern daybreaks are dazzling and peaceful, an inexorable reminder that yesterday has gone and the world marches on, erasing yesterday's pain without regret. At the end of my run, the sun rises high with the blinding promise of a new day.

Today school was back in session, and the way to work was littered with school buses and minivans, smiling moms and bus drivers welcoming the tiniest of students after a long day of elementary school at each bus stop along the way.

By 6:00 p.m. the Flamingo Lounge was already buzzing. The couches were full of men from the state attorney's office. They were drinking Maker's Mark Kentucky bourbon whisky, neat. I was told to just leave the bottle and walk away.

Old man Wilcox took his usual seat at the bar.

"Hello, Willy. Buffalo Trace and a splash of water?" I asked.

"You got it, pretty lady," he said.

After serving his drink, I asked, "Ready for a new magic trick?"

"Only if I can tell a dirty joke."

"I can't wait," I said.

I picked up my deck of cards and pulled out all four aces and the queen of hearts. "This trick is called the vanishing queen," I said. I placed two of the aces in my left hand, then the queen, then the two other aces, so that the queen was nestled nicely in the middle. I shuffled the cards a few times, turned them over one by one, and, "Voilà," I said. No queen, just aces. "Do you want me to bring her back?" I asked.

"Of course," he said.

I blew on the cards, shuffled them, turned them over one by one, four aces, and the queen reappeared.

"Amazing, Selena. Great sleight of hand."

"It's not sleight of hand, Willy. It's magic," I said.

"My turn," he said. "What is the difference between hungry and horny?"

"Hmm, I don't know. What?"

"Where you put the cucumber," he said, laughing out loud at his own joke. "I heard that on a podcast today."

"I love it," I said.

Renata arrived shortly after. "How was your day, Renata?" I asked while preparing her preferred drink, the Mary Pickford.

"Boring," she said while pulling out Swedish Fish from a Ziploc bag in her purse to pair with her drink. "Just had to defend a DUI today in court—the mayor's son."

"Really?"

"I don't know why I have to waste my time in court with his ongoing shenanigans. The judges just demand a small fine and let him walk away."

"Doesn't seem fair," I said.

"Well, when you have money and privilege, there is almost nothing you can't get away with," she said.

"You got that right," said Willy.

"Still, it's a win in my column, but secretly I wish he would get reprimanded in a way that would change his behavior for the safety of the public," said Renata. "It's exhausting to be his attorney."

At 7:00 p.m. a young, dark-haired, handsome man in his mid-twenties arrived.

"Hey, stranger," said Renata. "Where have you been all summer?"

"Slash, we've missed you around here," said Willy. "We thought you met some Madonna wannabe and abandoned us."

"No such luck," said Slash. "I have been teaching summer classes abroad on a cruise ship, Semester at Sea. I taught an international music class on board, and we stopped off at a few ports in Europe to help teach my students about music culture in each country, comparing their origins to today's music in the United States. A very unique adventure, which I enjoyed, but I won't soon volunteer for another semester. Six weeks traveling on a cruise ship took its toll on my body. I have been back for over a week now and still feel a bit queasy as the earth continues to sway under my feet."

"Slash," I said, "I am Selena. I just started here a few weeks ago. It's a pleasure to meet you. If you don't mind, I can offer a perfect cocktail concoction to help get you grounded. I'll make you a frozen ginger-pear bourbon martini."

"Sounds great," he said.

In the blender, I added ice, three slices of a pear, a sliver of ginger, 1 ounce of Cock'n Bull ginger beer, a splash of Sprite, and 3 ounces of Old Fitzgerald Kentucky bourbon. After blending, I poured this frozen delight into one of our extra large twenty-five-ounce martini glasses, especially suited for a frozen cocktail. I garnished the glass with a slice of pear and sprinkled a bit of cinnamon in the center.

"Amazing—almost too pretty to drink," said Slash.

"I am confident you will feel much better after a few sips."

"Thank you," said Slash sincerely.

"Slash is a very unusual name. Is that your nickname?"

"My name is Slash Stevens, and no, it is not my nickname but rather my official name. My parents had, well, still have a peculiar obsession with all things eighties. They were, and are still, big fans of eighties rock. Especially Guns N' Roses."

"So interesting. You don't look the part though. You look more like an actor from a soap opera than a rock band musician."

"Thank you for that. My parents' love of music did rub off on me though. There is no genre of music I don't enjoy, except maybe country music—Yuck! You know, everything you need to learn about love can be found in eighties rock lyrics."

"Really?" I asked.

"Really," he said. "I'll sing you a special thank you for helping me today." He started to sing:

"You're the reason I live
You're the reason I die
You're the reason I give when I break
down and cry
Don't need no reason why
Baby, baby, baby
You're my angel
Come and save me tonight"

"That's 'Angel' by Aerosmith—1988, I think," said Renata excitedly, as if she'd guessed the winning question on *Jeopardy*.

"Very good," said Slash.

"You get pretty good at this after a while. Slash loves to sing around here, and we pretty much all grew up in the eighties, or our parents did. Well, except maybe Willy," said Renata.

"Eighties music is full of untalented girly boys who can't sing," said Willy. "The true lyricists and most talented singers were in the sixties and seventies, like the Beatles, the Doors, the Carpenters, Janice Joplin, and Jimi Hendrix. It is a shame drugs and alcohol took so many of these artists too soon."

"Too soon indeed," I said. You're my angel, I thought. I am anything but. I ended a man's life and got fired from my career, but today someone appreciates me. I couldn't help but smile as my heart filled with a tiny bit of joy—something I had not felt in quite some time. Suddenly I was grateful to make a difference in someone's life, however small it may be. That day, I felt as though maybe, just maybe, I was turning the corner to a new beginning.

Chapter Twelve

Her

For Leslie, every morning starts off the same. She walks the property. Leslie starts her inspection by walking around the lobby, then through the restaurants, meeting and banquet spaces, the kitchen, and all guest hallways on twenty floors. Up and down every elevator, she writes copious notes. Leslie writes pages and pages of notes. She prepares a litany of items and areas that need immediate attention. Paint is chipped here, carpeting is dirty there, written comments about uniforms, old furniture that needs repair or needs to be replaced, and light fixtures that need dusting. She reports squeaky bell carts, dirty windows, and elevator doors that slam shut too quickly.

Leslie hears the employees chattering when she passes by. They say, "Oh no, it's *her*, watch out," or "Shit, put that away, it's *her*," or something to that effect. They don't call her by name. She is just known as *her*.

Everything changed once she arrived. The first change was the uniforms. She insisted upon a more professional look for staff. No more resort casual but rather classic pinstripe suits with skinny ties, a throwback to the times of Prohibition. The ladies were in white blouses with big classic bows and slim, figure-hugging skirts that fall four to six inches below the knee. It took a while for the staff to adjust to the new look, but it was more fitting for a hotel as exquisite as the Opulence Resort & Spa and its five-star, four-diamond status.

Leslie fired the sauté chef (sauces), poissonier chef (fish), entremetier chef (vegetable), and patissier chef (pastry), replacing them with young graduates of Florida's Johnson & Wales University, and recruited the executive chef from Palm Beach's illustrious Breakers hotel.

Her vision was to bring back some of the foods of yesteryear and pair them with today's current food trends. She wanted to bring back and elaborate on some of the more popular foods of the Great Depression and upgrade these dishes to a five-star experience. One of her ideas was to add shepherd's pie to the menu—a true favorite for families hit with hard times. She wanted chicken pot pies made larger and served in a cast iron skillet, also offering a vegetarian option by replacing the chicken with tofu.

Another big idea was transforming "Hoover stew," named after the thirty-first president, Herbert Clark Hoover. What was once macaroni, hot dogs, stewed tomatoes, and corn would be transformed into rotelle pasta, prosciutto Italian ham, white corn, peas, San Marzano peeled tomatoes, and spinach in a delicate white Alfredo sauce.

She didn't want to skimp on the prized menu items like surf and turf. She wanted large, two-pound lobsters, precracked and doused in butter, and fourteen ounces of filet mignon. She believed all items on the menu should be fit for a king, and the prices, of course, would reflect it, knowing full well that people would be delighted to pay any amount of money for such exquisite meals.

Leslie redecorated the two-story owner's suite by matching the sleek and modern style of the hotel's world-renowned executive suite. The executive suite was most notable for its famous and infamous guests, and custom fitted with an elevator, security cameras, and a hidden staircase for easy access to and from the suite for the purposes of escaping paparazzi and increased safety for dignitaries. Leslie was so intrigued by the infamy of this suite that she wanted the owner's suite to match its unique design. Because Leslie did not have office space within the building, she built an office within her suite. Upon returning to her suite in the evenings, she was often greeted with turndown service, which included a beautifully wrapped gold chunk of Baratti & Milano Italian chocolate or a bottle of sparkling wine on ice.

Today, however, she was greeted with a blue Tiffany box. When she held it in her hand, it vibrated slightly, nearly bouncing out of her palm, and she could hear a ticking sound. She hurriedly called security, who then called the Palm Beach police, who sent over the bomb squad. A big spectacle was created within the hotel. All staff and guests were detained outside in the parking lot, waiting to see what the whole debacle was about.

The bomb squad returned and reported that their robot had detected a very small explosive—a prankster bomb—inside the Tiffany box. The tiny explosive had just enough power to slightly burn your hands or face after opening, but it was not deadly.

Someone clearly has it out for me, Leslie thought. Whoever this is better watch out—because this bitch don't play.

Chapter Thirteen

Selena & The Bachelor Party

It was the night before Halloween, and today Salami was the first to arrive.

"You are here early," I said. "What is going on tonight?"

"*Buona sera*," he said. "Tonight we expect a nightcap visit from a bachelor party. One of our state senator's daughters has a VIP status event. The wedding is tomorrow, on Halloween, but tonight the bachelor party bus will end their evening's festivities here. So, needless to say, my services have been requested by management and the owners."

Salami put his earbuds back in his ears as he lumbered toward the back entrance where he stationed himself until needed, diligently learning Italian to prepare for his upcoming trip to Sicily. Every once in a while I could hear him talking to himself: "*Ciao, come stai*," or "*Lei, parla inglese*," which mean "Hello, how are you?" and "Do you speak English?" as far as I could tell from my mediocre comprehension from high school Italian.

You wouldn't necessarily know it was Halloween weekend at the Flamingo because the speakeasy never decorated for any special occasion. It was an entity all to itself. Any ghost or bat decoration found here would have Leslie or Talia's head spinning.

The evening started out slow, no visit from old man Wilcox or Renata, but Slash arrived shortly after opening.

"Hey, Selena," he said. "I heard there will be a crowd of pretentious, spoiled bastards here later this evening."

"That is what I heard from Salami. No one tells me anything around here. Why is that?"

"No idea. You should ask your sister Talia about that. All of us locals get a text alert about any interesting activities," he said.

"Interesting. I will have to ask her about that," I said. "I suppose that is why there is no sign of Willy or Renata today."

"Yeah, you are probably right. No one really wants to be witness to that shit show," he said.

"So why are you here?" I asked.

"Where there is a bachelor party there are sure to be a few beautiful tipsy women. I have a way with tipsy women. I am usually a reliably safe ride home," he said with a wink.

"Well, I hope you are not taking advantage of women in such a precarious state," I said.

"Never, not me. I met my last two girlfriends at bars, saving them from the dregs of society."

"Oh my, a real Prince Charming," I said with a friendly snicker.

"I would like to think so," he said seriously. I really do think that he thinks of himself in that way.

"I will keep you in mind the next time I am in danger," I said jokingly.

"You can count on me," he said. "Tonight, I am just going to stick with beer, in case my services are rendered."

"Yuengling, coming right up."

About an hour after opening, a young girl with long brown wavy hair, in an elegant, formfitting cocktail dress, sauntered into the speakeasy and sat beside Slash to his left.

"Hello, stranger," she said to Slash.

"What are you doing here? Didn't you graduate medical school in May? Shouldn't you be working twenty-four-seven in resident training?"

"That is a lot of questions," she said. "Yes, I graduated, yes I am currently a resident, but I am meeting a client here tonight. Mr. Lee. You remember him, right?"

"I thought you gave up that lifestyle now that med school is over," he said.

"Well, I did, but I like this client. I have been with him for five years now, so I think I will continue to see him," she said. "I miss him."

Slash started singing a John Waite song from 1984:

> *"I spend my time*
> *Thinking about you*
> *And it's almost driving me wild*
> *And that's my heart that's breaking*
> *Down this long distance line tonight*
> *I ain't missing you at all"*

"Very funny, Slash, except that I am missing him," she said.

"Be careful, Lila—please."

"Hello," I said. "My name is Selena." I stretched out my hand to shake hers. "What can I get for you this evening?"

"I'll have a French 75, please."

I hadn't made one of those yet, so I looked it up in the bartender's bible. In a shaker, I added ice, 1 ounce of gin, .5 ounces of lemon juice, 2 dashes of simple syrup, and 4 ounces of champagne, shook and strained it into a champagne flute, then garnished it with a lemon wheel.

"Perfect," she said. She took a sip and said, "Delicious. Thank you."

Slash explained, "Selena, Lila used to work here a few nights a week as a professional escort to help pay for medical school and, though she should be retired, is meeting Mr. Lee tonight. He will enter through the back door. Salami will let him in. He likes a drink called 'Between the Sheets' because, well—I am sure you can appreciate the humor. Look it up in the bible and just have it ready for him when he arrives. He is pretty picky, but a great tipper."

"Thanks for the heads-up," I said.

"Selena," Lila said, "one more thing. All of the regulars around here have a safe word, just in case they need help."

"A safe word?"

"Yes. If anyone orders an old-fashioned with extra cherries, that means HELP!"

"Duly noted. Thank you. I hope I never have to hear that," I said.

"You won't hear those words from me, Mr. Lee is a sweetheart," said Lila. Slash snickered and let out a long sigh while picking at the label affixed to his lager.

At 9:00 p.m. Mr. Lee arrived. Lila stood up from her barstool to hug him, and he kissed her gingerly on her cheek. As they settled in, I quickly put together his cocktail. In a shaker, I added ice, 1 ounce of Maison Gautier cognac, 1 ounce of light Bacardi rum, 1 ounce of triple sec, and .5 ounce of lemon juice, shook, and strained it into a chilled cocktail glass. I placed it on a purple cocktail napkin next to Lila.

"Hello," said Mr. Lee. "Whom do I have the pleasure of meeting this evening?"

"Hello," I said. "I am Selena. I am new here, and welcome."

"Thank you for having my drink ready for me. I truly appreciate it," he said.

"My pleasure," I said. "Tell me a secret, and I'll show you a magic trick."

"Hmm, a secret. That's precocious of you to ask; let me think." After a full minute of waiting silently, he said, "Alright, I have two secrets for you. The first one—like you said, it's a secret. I am thinking of buying this hotel from under the beast that is currently running it—you know *her*."

"I do know *her*, and your secret is safe with me," I promised. My mind was abuzz. WOW, I wonder if Talia has any inkling. I know she hates her. This secret is a bombshell.

"The second one," he said with a smile he could not hold back, "is that I am in love with this woman. Please take special care of her in my absence."

"Will do," I said.

As promised, it was my turn to show him a magic trick. I took out my deck of cards. "Pick a card, look at it, and put it back on top of this deck," I said. He took a card from the middle of deck, looked at it, showed Lila and Slash the card he chose, then placed it on top of the deck. I shuffled the deck three times, chose a card from the middle of the deck, and showed him the card.

"Is this your card?" I asked.

"No," he said.

Then I showed him the card on the bottom of the deck and asked, "Is this your card?"

"No," he said.

I then feigned a perplexed look upon my face and said, "How about this: look under your cocktail napkin." He lifted his cocktail, looked under his napkin—and there, looking straight at him, was the queen of hearts.

"Excellent," he said. "You will have to show me how you did that trick."

"It's not a trick," I said. "It's magic."

At 10:00 p.m., as the party bus arrived, Mr. Lee paid his tab in a hurry by tossing three hundred-dollar bills on the bar counter, the way Hollywood actors pay their tabs on television and in the movies. He then gently took Lila's arm, and the two of them walked out the back entrance past a gang of drunk imbeciles hugging each other, barely able to stand up straight. Holy shit, I thought, here we go. Maybe I won't have to serve them. They already look pretty wasted.

The least drunk of this reckless bunch approached the bar. "Hello. I am Jeff, and I would like to apologize now for all of my friends' behavior. This is a bachelor party for my friend Sam, who is marrying State

Senator Riley's daughter Amanda tomorrow evening. We are a rowdy bunch, but I am sure we will just have one round of shots before heading up to our rooms to bed before tomorrow's festivities," he said, looking exhausted.

"Excellent," I said. "What can I get for all of you?"

"For now, how about twelve Coors, and then we will decide what the last shot will be," he said.

"Twelve? I only see eight of you," I said.

"Oh, we have four lady friends getting off the bus right now."

"Bingo," said Slash.

"You are too much!" I said to Slash as Jeff walked away to join his friends and fellow groomsmen.

The boys returned to collect their beers. "Which one of you is the groom?" I asked.

"That is him over there." One of the boys pointed to a handsome, dark-haired man. "That's Sam. He is talking on his phone to his fiancé, probably trying to convince her that we weren't hooking up with prostitutes. Sad, really. Those two do not trust each other at all. I give them one year before they get divorced," he said.

"He has good reason not to trust her though. She threw herself at me just last week," another boy said.

"What the fuck!" said another one of the boys.

"Yeah, last week at the Gator game. She cornered me by the bathrooms."

"No shit?" said a groomsman.

"No shit!" he said, and suddenly they all seemed to sober up a bit.

"She cornered me, put her hands in my pants, and pulled me into one of the ladies' stalls. I tried to stop her, but I could not resist. I'm weak, and she's beautiful. I think I am going to tell him. I can't keep this secret any longer. She's a slut." The boy started to sweat, large beads forming on his forehead.

"Fucking asshole. Tim, you cannot tell him. He is going to get married tomorrow," said Jeff.

"Yes, I am," Tim said. "She is *my* old girlfriend. She should have married *me*."

"No, you are not telling him," another boy said. "She is happy with Sam. You had your chance, and you fucked it up."

At this point, I was starting to get angry. He was blaming the girl? I hardly believed his side of this story and wondered if it was true at all. I felt a vein throbbing in my right temple, took a deep breath, and told myself to remain calm. This was not my fight. I am just a bartender. I am trying to turn over a new leaf. No more rage and fight but rather I will take the advice of my sisters on how to handle a formidable adversary— revenge. Even though it was not actually *my* revenge, I felt compelled to keep this wedding on track. If this jerk were to railroad the wedding tomorrow and I didn't do anything about it, my sister would be pissed. The wedding could not be cancelled.

I chimed in at this point and said, "Hey, guys, how about a shot to celebrate? I'll create something just for this special occasion." While I was making shots for this pack of unruly wolves, four lovely ladies entered the speakeasy and found their way to the bar and sat next to Slash.

Slash chitchatted with the four of them. I could hear Slash say to one of the girls, "Hey, angel, are you lost? Because heaven is a long way from here." The girl just laughed, and I gave Slash a side-eye and shook my head. But it worked. Those two flirted back and forth, cozying up to one another very quickly and, as promised, before long they were holding hands. They said their good nights, and while they walked toward the door, I could hear him sing sweetly a 1984 song by Lisa Lisa & Cult Jam:

> *"I wonder if I take you home*
> *Will you still be in love baby*
> *Because I need you tonight"*

In the meantime, I made a batch of what I call the "dirty bastard," not from the bartender's bible but rather from my previous bartender days while attending college. In three of my largest shakers, I added ice, Bushmill's Original Irish whiskey, lime juice, ginger beer, and ginger syrup. I shook and strained the concoction into shot glasses. Then I made a special shot for Tim, that asshole trying to ruin the wedding. For him I mixed Baileys with lime juice, commonly known in the bartender trade as a "cement mixer." I handed the shots one by one to each of these slugs and then the special shot to Tim.

Jeff, the sober one, made a toast. "To Sam. May 'for better or worse' be far better than worse." And with that toast, they all slammed their shots.

Tim then said, "I have something I need to say." I just waited patiently for the cement mixer to kick in. It only takes a minute or two. Just as everyone's attention turned to asshole Tim, he turned to his left and puked, then knelt down on the floor, and I could almost hear the rumbling sound in his stomach. He shit himself right there, and just like that . . . crisis averted!

Chapter Fourteen

Selena & The Caretaker

As I was cleaning up from the evening's mischief, Hubert, the caretaker, appeared from the back of the room.

"Hello, my dear," he said.

I jumped, holding my heart, and turned toward him swiftly. "You scared me. Don't sneak up on me like that. What are you doing here so late at night?" I asked.

"I am just checking up on you to see how you are liking it here and to thank you for helping to avert a disaster with that Timothy fellow."

"How did you know about that?" I asked.

"I know everything that goes on around here," he said. "Thanks again. If that wedding got cancelled, it would not be good for the senator, his daughter, or the hotel."

"Well, I hope that boy recovers well from that cement mixer," I said.

"You don't have to worry about him. Mr. Salamoni has taken him home to his parents' house, and unfortunately, he will not be attending tomorrow's festivities."

"Oh, good grief," I said, mimicking one of my mother's favorite sayings. It's funny how your parents slip out sometimes unexpectedly.

I turned to grab my purse from behind the bar, and when I turned back around, Hubert was gone—again. This man was a far better magician than I could ever hope to be.

Chapter Fifteen

Her

Leslie, her brain still reeling from disbelief about the bomb attempt the night before, demanded additional cameras be installed on her floor and above her door to record everyone on their way in and out of the owner's suite.

She turned to Zander and asked, "Was it you? Are you trying to kill me?"

"Me? Why would I want to kill you?"

"For the money of course, and the hotel, the real estate, and the vineyard. Please tell me it wasn't you!"

"It was not me," Zander said reassuringly while rubbing his hands along her back and shoulders. "Please, Leslie, settle down. We will get to the bottom of this. Everything is going to be just fine. It was just a prankster bomb, not meant to hurt you. The police will figure this out. I promise," he said.

By 5:00 p.m. Leslie was still feeling unsettled, so she made her way over to the speakeasy. Old man Wilcox was sitting at the bar, and she was the second to arrive. She sat next to the old man, ordered a glass of Bordeaux, and asked Selena, "Do you want to know another secret?"

"Of course," said Selena.

"I think Zander is trying to kill me."

"Are you talking about the prank in your suite?"

"Yes."

"Don't you think you are being a bit overly dramatic? I mean, I heard that the bomb was not intended to hurt someone, and if you don't mind me saying, Zander seems a little wimpy. Do you really think he could pull off a murder?" I asked.

"Well, he almost raped your sister," she said.

"The way I understand it is that the necktie incident was a miscommunication. Some of the asshole men my sister worked with set her up by telling Zander she liked rough sex," I said.

"It worked out great for her, didn't it? A promotion and then promoted again to general manager," she said.

"The second promotion had to do with helping unmask the murderer of the former general manager's wife, who plunged to her death from an eighth-floor balcony. Well, that's a long story for another day. The general manager's secretary, Janine, and his daughter, Gracie, wrote a screenplay and book about it. *The Executive Suite.* You should read it. You know, it worked out great for you too. You've got Zander, and no, I don't think he is trying to kill you. He doesn't seem the type."

"I've got Zander?" Leslie said. "Our relationship is quite complicated, but similar to Talia's story in the executive suite, it's a long story for another day."

Old man Wilcox said, "If I were going to kill you, I would poison you slowly."

"Really? And how would you do that, old man?" she asked.

"Oh, I don't know," said Willy. "Maybe spike your wine every day with a little poison that would, over time, mimic a stroke. Isn't that how one of your husbands died?"

"Bite your tongue you old bag of farts, or you won't see your next birthday," said Leslie. "I guess when you're a hundred years old, you are not afraid to say just about anything."

"Are you flirting with me?" mused Willy. "The way I understand it, I am just your type—old and half dead already."

She gave Willy a hardened look, trying to look stern, but unexpectedly gave into laughter. "Willy, you are something else. God love ya!"

Zander arrived shortly after and sat next to Leslie. He pulled a small green Gatorade bottle out of his jacket pocket. "Do me a favor?" he asked Selena. "Keep this in the refrigerator for me. No one knows this, but I have low blood sugar and this Gatorade is mixed with medicine. Keep it here just in case I need it."

"My pleasure," said Selena. "Your secret is safe with me."

Chapter Sixteen

Selena

The weather in Palm Beach in November is nearly perfect. Seventy-five to eighty degrees in the daytime, and the temperature falls into the high sixties or low seventies by nightfall.

Because I only live a mile or so away from the hotel, I have been walking to and from work lately. I am not the paranoid type, and although I am not a police officer anymore, I can't ignore my inner cop telling me to watch out. Nearly every time I walk along South Ocean Boulevard or the boardwalk, I get a strange feeling that I am being watched. Sometimes I turn around abruptly, just to be sure, but no one is ever there—well, maybe just a few unfortunate homeless souls along the park path. I often bring a few of the ladies food from the hotel at the end of my shift or hand out any spare change left behind from bar patrons after they pay their tabs. No one really cares for coins these days. They jingle in your pocket, they're heavy, and they usually just get left behind, which I don't mind. My friends in the park can make good use of it, whatever they choose to use that money for—no judgement. Living in the streets is a hard life.

One afternoon on the way to work, I stopped to chat with Jenny, a homeless woman who sometimes sleeps in the park gazebo with her cat.

"Hello, Jenny," I said. "How are you today? If you are around later this evening, I can bring you some leftovers from the bar."

"I would love that," she said. "Can I ask you something?"

"Sure," I said.

"Who is that lady who is always following you?"

"What lady?" I asked, almost frantically.

"Oh, I don't want to upset you," she said. She turned and started to walk away. She repeated to herself, "Don't upset Selena. Don't upset Selena. Mind your own business."

"Jenny, please tell me. What did you see?" I asked while following her as she was walking away abruptly.

"Well, there is a woman. She is small, maybe a teenager. She follows you sometimes. Haven't you noticed?"

"No," I said.

"Watch out, Selena," said Jenny. "I will pray for you today." Then she repeated, "Pray to God. Pray to God. Protect Selena. God, Selena is good. Selena is my friend."

"Thank you, Jenny," I said sincerely. "Thank you for looking out for me."

"That is what friends do," said Jenny.

"Yes, that is what friends do," I said. After walking away, I could still hear Jenny say, "Friends are good. Friends are good. Jenny and Selena are friends."

Chapter Seventeen

Her

Thanksgiving week, Leslie and Zander decided to embark upon a twelve-day European cruise, leaving Talia in charge of all decision-making. Their departure from the hotel was quite a sight to behold. The bellman pushed three luggage carts brimming with seven designer suitcases, an array of coats for all kinds of weather, a tuxedo bag, and an elongated garment bag full of designer evening gowns.

She was followed by Zander, trailing behind her like a cocker spaniel, and two large male security guards with earpieces so they could communicate with—who knows? She seldom went anywhere without security after the "attempted bombing," as she preferred to call it. A bit overly dramatic, but that was just Leslie's way. She loves all of the attention and trusts no one. Within minutes, her Bentley stretch limousine pulled under the porte-cochère and, with the help of three bellmen, off they went.

That same afternoon, Mr. Lee arrived with a team of men and women in suits holding clipboards. They stood silently in the middle of the lobby, waiting for direction from Mr. Lee, as the hotel staff stared at them in bewilderment.

"Alright, team. You know your assignments. Let's meet back here in precisely one hour," said Mr. Lee, a short, portly Asian man who seemed determined to complete an important mission that no one and nothing could alter. His team combed every speck of the hotel: the lobby, front desk, banquet halls, kitchen, and a few available suites. They chatted with hotel staff, mid-level management, Human Resources, and hotel security. By the time the grandfather clock in the lobby chimed three times, almost one hour after they arrived, they had all completed their tasks. In the same manner in which they'd arrived, in a flurry, was the same way they departed, leaving everyone who witnessed this strange event scratching their heads.

Talia knew that Leslie would be livid if she knew what had transpired here over the past hour or so, but she remembered Leslie's last words before she left: "Don't fucking call me. I am on vacation. Don't call me for any reason, at all, unless there is blood involved." Technically, no blood was shed—so no call was made.

Chapter Eighteen

Selena

One of the things I love most about Thanksgiving week is that I get to see my nephew, Talia's ten-year-old son, Patrick. He attends a boarding school in Sarasota, and although Talia travels north to spend most weekends with him, Patrick only flies home to Palm Beach a few times a year: Thanksgiving, Christmas, spring break, and summer.

At the speakeasy, old man Wilcox, Renata, and Slash arrived one right after the other. I was preparing Slash's cocktail when a small figure entered the room. It was Patrick.

"Hey, Aunt Selena," he said.

"Hey, sweetie," I said and ran out from behind the bar to give him a giant bear hug. "I really missed you. I can't believe it has been three months since I have seen you last. I can't wait to hear all about school. But first, how did you get in here?"

"I followed him," he said and pointed his finger at Slash. "He pressed the letter *A* and the number 3 on the jukebox and went behind the curtain, so I did the same. I love this secret entrance thing, very cool."

"Hey, stalker, now you know my code song to get in," said Slash.

"Yeah, 'Don't You Want Me' by the Human League," said Patrick with disgust.

"Seems fitting," said Renata.

"Definitely," I said.

"Stupid song," said Patrick.

"Well, it was very popular in 1981, kid," said Slash, defending his choice of secret theme song.

"Be careful what you say around Patrick, guys. He is Talia's kid. He's pretty sharp and has eyes in the back of his head," I said.

Patrick smiled and said, "Okay, Aunt Selena, show me one of your terrible magic tricks. Let me see if you have gotten any better."

"Terrible?" said Willy. "I think she is pretty talented."

"Well, you must be blind then. I can see right through her card tricks from a mile away."

"I have to agree with you there, kiddo. These old eyes don't work like they used to," said Willy.

I took out my deck of cards and spread the cards out on the bar, facing up, so everyone could see all the cards. Then I said, "I'll bet if I throw all of these cards at the mirror above the liquor bottles, I can get only the queen of hearts to land right side up and stick somewhere on the mirror."

"Okay," everyone chimed in.

I turned around, threw a whole deck of cards at the mirror, and at first glance, none of the cards landed right side up and no card seemed to stick. After a closer look, behind the Bacardi light rum, the queen of hearts stared back at us. All of the other cards landed somewhere along the bar or floor, face down.

"Spectacular," said Willy.

"Great job, Selena," said Renata.

Slash just looked bewildered.

"That is your worst trick yet," said Patrick. "When you turned around, you grabbed another deck from your pocket, threw that deck at the mirror, and all of the cards in that deck have the back side printed on both sides. I bet you placed the queen of hearts on the mirror before everyone arrived here tonight. Very clever, but a very easy trick."

"Okay, you little shit, no more tattletaleing, and give Slash his watch back."

"Alright," said Patrick.

"First you steal my theme song, then my watch? What is wrong with this kid?" said Slash. "You're a pesky little shit."

"What are they teaching you in this boarding school?" asked Renata.

"I learned all of my tricks from the tricksters and thieves in my family: my grandmother, my mom, and my aunts.

"Hey, don't be telling all our family secrets," I said, "or I am going to have to kick you out of here. You are not good for business."

Soon after, Talia walked into the speakeasy. "There you are, Patrick. I was looking all over for you," said Talia. "Are you hungry? Let's go get something to eat."

"Why can't I stay here? I can order food from room service and eat it here," cried Patrick.

"Well, you can't," said Talia adamantly.

"Why not?"

"Because you are ten! For Christ's sake, Patrick, let's go!"

"I love that kid," said Willy.

"Me too," Renata and Slash chimed in.

Chapter Nineteen

Her

When the cruise ship left port, Leslie was reminded about the wisdom of Anne Lamott, American novelist and political activist. She said, "Almost everything will work again if you unplug it for a few minutes . . . including you."

It had been years since Leslie had been able to sneak away for a vacation, let alone one where her cell phone worked sparingly, and not at all while deep at sea. She thoroughly enjoyed her vacation with Zander and enjoyed having the ability to unplug and unwind. She wished she had more opportunities to whisk off and enjoy herself more often. She made a note to herself to take more vacations in the new year and find time to enjoy her wealth that she worked so hard to acquire.

Upon arrival at the port in Barcelona twelve days later, her cell phone chimed incessantly with text messages, many of which read: *Emergency, please call* or *Hotel*

911 or *Call me as soon as you get off the ship.* The numerous text messages sent to her phone came from many different people: her real estate attorney, Anna, Talia's secretary, and hotel security.

Leslie played a few of her voice mails as soon as she was able, then screamed out, "Motherfucker!"

Chapter Twenty

Selena

Everyone at the Opulence hotel was walking on eggshells when the news broke that Leslie would be back home within the hour. Housekeeping and banquet staff were out in full force, cleaning all areas from the hotel entrance to the back parking lot. Hotel staff worked diligently to get the hotel pristinely clean, hoping to escape Leslie's wrath.

I was already working behind the bar when Leslie entered the lobby. I figured whatever was going on out there was none of my business.

Willy arrived on time, and today I was really happy to have someone to talk to right away in case Leslie worked her way back here and I would have to listen to her rant on about how Mr. Lee was trying to buy this hotel out from under her, all the while pretending I didn't know this was going to happen.

"Hello, Willy," I said.

"Hello, pretty lady," he said. "All hell seems to be breaking loose out there. Leslie is on a tirade in the lobby, angrily yelling at everyone."

"Mmm hmm," I said. "I am trying to stay out of that."

"You remember what Mr. Lee said weeks ago, right?"

"Yes, I do, and I don't think that this is going to play out very well. She is going to be pissed off," I said. "Buffalo Trace on the rocks?"

"Yes, ma'am."

"Willy, all this time I have been serving you, I never asked what it is you did for a living before retiring. It suddenly dawned on me that I know very little about you," I said.

"Yeah, no one ever really chats with the old man at the bar," he said. "In a way, I like the anonymity of that. I will enlighten you with my past but not before a magic trick and a joke."

"Alright," I said. I took out three red Solo cups from a drawer behind the bar, and I showed him three red balls. I placed one red ball under each of the cups. I moved the cups around each other, many times, masquerading movement and misdirection. I lifted up the cup to his left. It was empty. I lifted up the cup to his right. It was empty. I lifted up the middle cup, and all three balls rolled out from under that cup.

"Excellent," he said. "Now put all the balls back where they belong."

"Of course," I said, and I put the three balls and the three cups back in my drawer behind the bar.

"That was not what I meant," he said.

"I know, but I haven't mastered customer requests yet," I said apologetically. "Your turn to tell me a joke."

"What is the difference between a tire and 365 used condoms?"

"I don't know. What?" I said with a shrug.

"One is a good year, and one is a great year."

"Very funny. I like that one," I said. "Now it is your turn to tell me a bit more about yourself. Are you married? Do you have any kids?"

"No, you first," he said.

"Okay. I am not married, no kids, do not have a boyfriend, and I am not looking for one."

"Why?" he asked.

"Well, it's like Maslow's hierarchy of needs. There are five levels of self-actualization or human happiness, but to get there you need to master each level or phase. The first level is food, water, and clothing. The next is safety, like your home or job. The third is finding compassionate friends and belonging to a community. I am currently happy here in this phase. I have a new job, I am making new friends, spending more time with my family, and until I am more comfortable with myself, here in this phase, I won't be ready to master the self-esteem necessary to move on to a more meaningful relationship to enter stage four. So, basically, I am just not ready yet."

"What do you see as stage five? What does true happiness mean to you?" he asked.

"Well, the final stage is when you actually feel that you are living the life you dreamed of, happy with all the choices you made along the way, waking up each morning and returning to bed each evening blissful."

"That is a great fairytale." His tone was polite, but I got the feeling he thought that Maslow's theory is all bullshit.

"Now it is your turn," I said with anticipation.

"Married once. She died twenty years ago, natural causes, in her sleep."

"I am sorry to hear that," I said.

"No kids," he said, "but just to be safe, I don't answer my phone on Father's Day."

"Very funny," I said with a laugh I could not hold back.

"What about your career?" I asked.

"If you must know, I used to be an investigative journalist for the *Miami Herald*."

"Really? That is so interesting." My eyes widened. Now he really had my attention.

"I mostly investigated cold cases in the late seventies. One of my cases was to look into the disappearance of a lounge entertainer here at the Opulence Resort."

"Tell me more," I said.

"Well, there were two disappearances actually. A woman and a bellman disappeared in the late forties, never to be heard from again. The rumor at the time was that she was dating one of the owners, and when they broke up suddenly, she started dating a bellman, but within a few weeks, she and the bellman both disappeared. The owner was known to have said something like, 'If you leave me, you may never see the light of day again.' I interviewed lots of staff members at the time, who were very difficult to track down thirty-some-odd years after their employment ended and the duo disappeared. Ultimately, I was told to walk away from the story."

"Did you?" I asked.

"I did."

"Why?"

"They paid me handsomely, and I needed the money. I did, however, keep all of my findings, and one day, when I die, I will have my attorneys hand it over to the police, but without the bodies, I doubt there is anything the police can do."

"Who are 'they,' and is there anything salacious in your reporting?"

"I don't know who 'they' are really. I was visited in my home by two lawyers, who handed me an envelope full of money. That is so cliché, but that is how things were done in those days. As far as salacious, the staff told me that periodically people would disappear, and there was a rumor circulating about an underground vault or tunnel around here that, if found, bodies would be found too."

"Fascinating," I said. "I am intrigued. I don't doubt it—this place has quite a few secret doors, staircases, and tunnels. No telling what secrets lie behind its walls or beneath the earth." I made a mental note to ask Hubert, the caretaker, about an underground vault the next time he magically appeared.

Chapter Twenty-One

Her

Shortly after Leslie arrived home from her whirlwind European adventure and verbally attacked hotel staff, she returned to the owner's suite. Within minutes, she was startled by a loud knocking at the door. When she opened the door, she was greeted by four men in suits.

"Are you Ms. Leslie Lewis?" one of the men asked.

"Yes, of course. Who else would live in the owner's suite?"

"These papers are for you," he said. The expressionless man turned and walked toward the elevator immediately after she snatched the manila envelope from his hand. The other men followed in unison.

She read the documents, then handed them to Zander to read. "What the fuck is going on?" she screeched.

"It looks like the silent partners of the property have sold a portion of their shares to Mr. Lee and offered him the position as managing director, thereby pushing you out as the current managing partner. It looks like you need to vacate the premises by the first of the new year, when this agreement will take effect."

"Do I have any say in this?" she asked. "What if I don't agree to this? We need to get our lawyers involved in this—and not a word to anyone until we figure this out."

"Leslie, please try to stay calm. It states here that you will keep all of your shares in the company. You just will not be allowed to manage the property. Think of it this way: you will keep your investment, but now you will not have to do any work. I don't necessarily see this as a bad thing. We can buy a home on the waterfront and travel more, like you said you wanted to. You know, enjoy life to the fullest. You don't need the stress of this full-time job. This could actually be a blessing. Maybe you could even start a family."

"I am forty-fucking-five years old, and do I look like a fucking mother to you?"

At closing time, Leslie arrived at the speakeasy.

"Hello, Leslie. I was just cleaning up. Can I get you a glass of Bordeaux?" asked Selena.

"Definitely," she said.

"You look like you had a rough day."

"I am exasperated and emotionally exhausted, if you couldn't tell," Leslie said with a heavy sigh. "I am sorry to burden you with my worries, but I really feel like you are my only friend around here, and we have only known each other for a few short months."

"Thank you for that," Selena said sincerely. "I'll bet you are still rattled about the prankster bomb and stressed about the potential takeover by Mr. Lee and his army of robot accountants."

"I'll bet that stupid bomb was Mr. Lee's idea of a joke," Leslie said. "Well, Mr. Lee," she muttered aloud as if he was in the room, "if you spent any time talking to my staff, you should already know you better WATCH OUT—they don't call me the 'harbinger of doom' for nothing."

Chapter Twenty-Two

Selena

Sugar and spice and everything nice, while cliché, is the best way to describe the Christmas season in Palm Beach. By the time December first rolls around, the Opulence Resort & Spa turns into a winter wonderland. The lobby welcomes guests with scents of gingerbread, hot cocoa, and Christmas cookies. Christmas music plays all day and throughout the night.

A full-sized gingerbread house is erected, copying the original idea from the Fontainebleau Resort in Miami Beach. This year's gingerbread house was crafted by Ms. Kate, our pastry chef, who studied her craft in Paris. This twenty-five-foot-tall completely edible two-story house was a Victorian masterpiece featuring ten windows, a multigabled roofline, large front porch, and fifteen-foot Christmas trees on either side. The entire estate was edible, including nutcracker soldiers, snowmen, and even Santa, a few elves, and Rudolph. More

than one thousand pounds of each ingredient
—honey, sugar, chocolate, flour—helped to
create this home, along with plenty of
gumdrops, candy canes, Hershey's kisses,
and gummy bears, which decorate its
interior and exterior walls. The colorful
candy sparkles and glistens as the sun shines
through the lobby windows. The price tag
for this creation was almost eighty thousand
dollars, but it was worth every penny, as this
magical wonderland brings with it plenty of
notoriety and hotel guests to offset the
whopping expense.

    The hotel brings in an electric
passenger train and merry-go-round for the
smallest children to enjoy. The kitchen staff
offers a complimentary cooking class for
older children to bake Christmas cookies in
the bakery, and a ten-foot mailbox stands by
the lobby entrance where guests can drop off
checks to donate to the Make-A-Wish
Foundation. Every year, the hotel collects
over one hundred thousand dollars for the
charity, and the hotel owners pledge to
match that amount from their own pockets
to double the donation amount. Who would
imagine Christmas in Florida could be so
spectacular. Santa himself visits the night
before Christmas Eve to make sure that the

last wishes of the children will not be forgotten.

December first also marks the day of the annual Palm Beach Realtor Association Christmas party. The evening starts off with photos in front of the gingerbread house, where they are greeted by elves who serve the guests with gingerbread cookie cocktails in oversized red Christmas mugs, which I whipped up shortly before they arrived.

After photos and a cocktail, the group will make their way into the speakeasy for a cocktail hour before their dinner in the Venetian ballroom on the fifth floor, overlooking the Atlantic Ocean with floor-to-ceiling windows.

On this day, Salami arrived donning a Santa hat with a large jingle bell nosily bouncing around as he ambled along.

"Cute getup," I said.

"*Buon Natale*," he said as he made his way to his usual perch in the back of the lounge.

None of my regulars showed up at opening today. I guess none of them are big fans of Realtors. There were, however, lots of beautiful young women, perfect for Slash I thought.

Since there were over two hundred Realtors and I only had them for one hour before they rode the elevators up to dinner, I prepared a preset bar menu. I premade large pitchers of a few specialty Christmas drinks. "Santa's Helper" included Captain Morgan spiced rum and Old New England eggnog with drizzled caramel sauce along the sides and bottom of the martini glasses and a few mini marshmallows to float on top. "The Santa" was actually a strawberry margarita rimmed with red sugar instead of salt. "The Grinch" was made with 2 ounces of vodka, 1 ounce of Midori liqueur, 1 ounce of pineapple juice, and a splash of Sprite in a martini glass rimmed with green sugar. I also offered, because it takes no additional preparation, champagne, wine, and beer. Before the hour was over, I produced over 350 drinks, and the tipsy Realtors left far happier than when they arrived.

Once the group departed, Slash arrived.

"You missed all the fun," I said.

"They will be back after the dinner. Trust me on that one. That dinner is full of brownnosing awards and accolades, and it won't be long before a bored, drunk group of lovelies returns."

"Really?" I said in a slight panic. "I am not really prepared for that. Look at this place. It's a mess."

"I'll help you clean up all of these glasses," he offered.

"Oh, no worries," I said. "I'll call the banquet department and ask for a small cleanup staff. I meant to ask you—how did it go with that girl you left with after the bachelor party?"

"Oh, her? She was a really sweet girl. We went out a few times, but she is not my type."

"Why?"

"She listens to country music," he said disappointedly.

"Ugh, that is the worst," I said. "Definite dealbreaker."

Talia arrived next, with Patrick. "Hey, you two," I said. "What do you have going on tonight?"

"We are going to the county fair to go on a few rides and eat carnival food—fun times," said Talia.

"I wish you could come," said Patrick.

"I am sorry. I have to work tonight, but let's plan some fun for Sunday, maybe a movie, or I heard there is a new laser tag place that just opened. Maybe we could go there."

"Sounds good," said Patrick.

"This place is a mess," said Talia.

"I know. I called banquets to send staff for cleanup," I said.

"Hey, stalker," said Slash. "How did you get in here this time?"

"My mom's song on the jukebox is much better than your sorry-ass song," said Patrick.

"Really? What is her theme song for entry?" I asked.

" 'Work Bitch' by Britney Spears," said Patrick.

"Well, of course that's her song. Very fitting," I said. "You two need a drink before you leave?"

"A Shirley Temple for Patrick and a shot of Jameson for me," said Talia. "It has been quite a day."

"What happened?" I asked.

"It has just been a stressful few days overseeing the building of the gingerbread house, giant Hanukkah candles, the carousel, et cetera, and we are nearly sold out for the entire month."

"That's great. Maybe that will keep Leslie off your back," I said.

"Yeah, right. The strange thing is that I haven't seen her or Zander much since they returned from their cruise a few days ago."

"She may not be the managing partner here any longer," said Patrick.

"What?" said Talia with alarm. "How do you know about that? How do you even know what a managing partner is?"

"I heard her talking on the phone in the elevator about someone named Mr. Lee and that she is supposed to move out by the end of the year. No one ever worries about being discrete with a kid around. I heard the whole damn thing."

"Language, Patrick."

"Okay, Mom."

"Good job, Patrick. Keep your ears open. That's a crazy story. I can't wait to hear more about it," said Talia. "Drink up. We gotta go."

They got up off the barstools to leave. While Talia said goodbye to me, Patrick patted Slash's shoulder to say goodbye to him.

"Patrick, give Slash his watch back," I said.

"Ugh, okay, Aunt Selena."

"Geez, kid, you're a menace," said Slash.

"Yeah, we sure are proud of him," said Talia.

The cleanup crew arrived, and within ten short minutes the lounge was back to its original state. These guys work like magic elves, I thought.

By 9:00 p.m. a group of ladies arrived back to the lounge from their Christmas party. As they were walking through the door, Slash said, "I told you."

"Lucky for you."

"Yes, indeed."

Before long, Slash was chatting with a young lady named Eileen, and I already knew what was going to come out of his mouth next. Slash started to sing the 1982 song "Come On Eileen" by Dexys Midnight Runners:

"Come on Eileen, oh I swear what he means
At this moment, you mean everything
You in that dress, my thoughts I confess
Verge on dirty, ah come on Eileen"

In the year 2021, most women would be offended by Slash's antics from anyone else, but he has such boyish charm that women just melt in his presence. Add in his good looks, great voice, the way he runs his fingers through his hair while watching your lips as you speak, and the world is his for the taking. Of course Eileen loved every minute of the attention, and of course Slash offered to drive her home safely. Always the hero.

By 11:00 p.m. the bar was empty. Salami said *"Buona notte,"* and walked out the back entrance. After cleaning and organizing the bar for the next day, I decided I would walk home to enjoy the cool December weather. When I got outside, I caught a glimpse of a woman staring at me from across the street, nicely dressed but with an eerie look upon her face. What happened next was just like a scene in a horror movie; a bus passed by and then, miraculously, she was gone. This gave me chills—the heebie-jeebies my grandma would say, a throwback to a 1956 song by Little Richard. Just to be safe, I called an Uber to bring me home.

Chapter Twenty-Three

Her

When bread becomes toast, it can never go back to being bread again. Once innocence is lost, it can never be recaptured. Once mistakes have been made, they can't be corrected. Leslie's life was forever changed with her parents' death. She was forced to fend for herself at the tender age of just fifteen years old. There would be no private school education, fancy clothes, or even a college degree in her future. She and her brother were left with no money, as all of the family finances were used to pay off her parents' debts. The house, cars, and jewelry were liquidated to pay off the bank loans. She had no idea that her dad had a gambling problem.

All of her childhood recollections were laced with happy memories of grand parties, exquisite vacations, fun family game nights, and lots of love. With no family members able to take her and her brother in, they were separated and sent off to be raised by strangers in the foster care system.

After the death of Leslie's first husband, she met Raymond, an elderly gentleman who had acquired his wealth the old-fashioned way—he was born into it. His family accrued millions working with Henry Flagler and the Rockefellers in the 1870s for Standard Oil Company. That poor son of a bitch had met his demise swimming off his beachfront property in Palm Beach a few years ago. Her neighbor showed up at the door to deliver the news of his drowning, dripping wet, distraught, and in tears. Her initial thought was that it could not have happened to a better man. He probably should not have drunk so much coffee before his morning swim. An elderly heart can only take so much exertion. His death left her with many more millions. The newspapers were never able to uncover the exact amount of money she obtained through his death, but the local reporters found pleasure in pinning her as a black widow of sorts because of her two elderly husbands who died in her care.

With such a terrible reputation, Leslie knew she needed to change the trajectory of her public persona, so she spent the next fifteen years creating an extensive portfolio of real estate ventures that included malls, a winery, and a five-star hotel, proving to the Palm Beach community that she should be respected as a formidable venture capitalist and member of Palm Beach's exclusive polite society.

A team of lawyers knocked on Leslie's door just a day after she was informed about Mr. Lee's imminent managing takeover of the Opulence Resort.

"It is about time you showed up. You better have some excellent ideas about what options I have in order to retain my managing directorship," she said defiantly.

"Maybe we should sit down to discuss this," one of the lawyers said.

"That sounds like bad news," she shot back. "It better not be bad news."

The four lawyers positioned themselves around the glass coffee table on two designer couches, shifting uncomfortably, looking dewy with droplets of sweat anxious to escape perfectly manicured hairlines. One of the lawyers was bald and had to seize a handkerchief from his back pocket in an effort to pat down the sweat emanating from his scalp. He rubbed the cloth over his head feverishly. "Is it hot in here?" he asked.

"No, not at all," she said in disgust.

"Ms. Lewis, the team and I have read through all of the paperwork, and it pains me to say that you have no legal recourse to continue your work here in your current capacity. I know this is difficult to hear, but Mr. Lee will be the new managing director and has requested that you surrender the owner's suite here at the Opulence Resort before the end of the year."

"I paid you a shit ton of money for you to just inform me that there is nothing I can do but move out and move on?"

"Yes, that is correct. You will still keep all of your shares in the ownership agreement. You just lose the residence and your job here at the hotel."

"When does this new contract actually take effect?"

"January first."

"So that means if I can change Mr. Lee's mind about the acquisition or if he changes his mind on his own, I have until January first before the agreement goes into effect. Is that correct?"

"Yes, that is correct, ma'am."

"Well, I will just have to find a way to change his mind and stop this takeover. Three weeks is a long time. Anything can happen in three weeks."

Chapter Twenty-Four

Selena

When I arrived home, my door was ajar. A tingling sensation climbed the back of my neck, and as it intensified, I took my revolver, a Ruger GP100, out of my backpack, a habit I started last week after Jenny, the homeless woman in the park, told me she thought someone might be following me. Whether the woman staring at me from the other side of the street tonight was real or imagined, I was startled and fearful of what I might find inside the apartment. The right thing to do would be to call 911 or my old partner, but I couldn't help myself. I had to know if someone was in my apartment now.

I held the gun in my right hand and stabilized it with my left as I opened the front door gingerly with my foot and entered the condo slowly, taking silent steps steadily, following the corridor to the kitchen. There in the center of the kitchen was a cake with white frosting, decorated elegantly with a green-and-red Christmas tree, that I did not bake. The largest knife from my knife block was protruding from the middle. A sliver of cake was missing, and a note was left on the kitchen island in red letters that read:

Sliced and devoured, revenge is sweet and best served cold.

Chapter Twenty-Five

Mr. Lee

When you love a woman, she becomes your favorite cocktail. She shines bright, lucid; like the moon and twinkling stars, she becomes a love song that replays in your head, then she turns into your whole world.

Mr. Lee awoke the morning of December seventeenth with only one goal in mind: how exactly to ask for Lila's hand in marriage. Maybe I'll ask her tonight at the speakeasy, the place we met for the first time five years ago, or maybe I'll ask her during a walk along the beach after dinner this evening, he thought. Where will we spend our honeymoon? Somewhere exotic for sure, maybe Paris or the Maldives or Venice. Wherever she decides, my heart will follow.

The four-carat marquise-cut diamond sparkled brilliantly, nestled comfortably in its iconic robin's-egg-blue Tiffany box. Mr. Lee sat at the kitchen table staring at the ring, the very instrument that would forever change his life, unwilling to put the lid back on the box. Because the excitement of this day was so grand, he wanted to make this moment of happiness last as long as possible.

As Mr. Lee was deciding what to wear that evening, his butler, James, entered the gentleman's quarters with a note and a black box. The black box with gold foil held within it Korean tea similar to the tea he once drank with his grandmother. What a delightful and thoughtful gift, he thought.

"James, where did this come from?"

"A courier just brought it by a few minutes ago."

"You know, sending someone Korean tea is a truce of sorts. Korean tea represents respect, harmony, and tranquility. A very thoughtful gift. I wonder whom it is from?"

Mr. Lee opened the note. It said:

Dear Mr. Lee,
Congratulations on your recent acquisition.

"Wonderful," said Mr. Lee.

"Was the note signed?" asked James.

"No. Strange, but a considerate cultural gift nevertheless. James, would you mind making a cup of tea for me while I dress?"

Chapter Twenty-Six

Selena & The Santa Wedding

The magic of Christmas sounds like jingle bells and smells like sugar cookies, but it is the warmth of the heart that sprinkles the magic of Christmas through the air. My favorite Christmas story that I must watch every year is *The Year Without a Santa Claus*. While the voice actors are long dead, their sentiment and joy of Christmas lives on. Snow Miser competes with the Heat Miser vying for Mother Nature's attention, and despite their differences, they decide to work together to make a joyful Christmas for children all over the world, notably portrayed by the little girl who writes a letter to Santa and sings about having a blue Christmas without a sick Santa. It makes me cry every single time. But it is the joy that warms my heart when Santa decides, after reading the letter, that there will be *no* year without a Santa Claus, that keeps me coming back year after year.

This evening would be the hotel's biggest wedding of the year, and wouldn't you know it, all attendees would be dressing in Santa-clad ensembles, with the bride and groom donning Mr. and Mrs. Santa attire. We were expecting about four hundred people. I couldn't think of a more photoworthy event for our public relations and advertising executives than a four-hundred-person-plus Santa-themed wedding.

At 5:00 p.m. Salami arrived and said, "*Buon Natale*," as he walked past the bar.

"Merry Christmas," I chimed back. Although, we still have eight days to go, but Merry Christmas season for sure. "What should we expect tonight?"

"We have the Santa wedding," he said, "and we expect about fifty to one hundred guests from the wedding party later this evening."

"Sounds fun. I will prepare a specialty drink for the occasion," I said. "Since they will come later this evening, I will prepare a dessert aperitif, a candy cane peppermint ensemble I think will fit the theme of the evening."

"*Bene*," he said, meaning "fine" or "okay," but I thought what he really meant was "so what" or "who cares." But I don't think he knows how to say that in Italian, and neither do I. Suddenly I wondered why I tried talking to him at all. I was sure that he couldn't care less.

Renata was the first to arrive today. "How are you, Selena? I hear we have a visit from Santa's village tonight."

"Well, more like Santa clones and less the rest of the village, like elves. I believe they were not invited."

"Wouldn't it be fun if the waiters and waitresses were dressed like elves though?"

"Great idea. I would tell Talia and Leslie but they are all about keeping up a five-star professional look and status. You can imagine."

"Yes, I can," she said. "Where is the old man?"

"Here I am," Willy said as he approached the bar.

"Jeez Louise, don't sneak up on people like that."

"Sorry," he said.

"Mary Pickford and a Buffalo Trace?" I asked. "Actually, on second thought, how about a specialty drink I am trying out for the Santa wedding tonight? If you two think it is good enough for prime time, then I will prepare a big batch for the wedding party stragglers."

"Okay, why not?" said Renata.

"Sure," said Willy.

I prepared in a shaker with ice, doubling the recipe: 2 ounces of strawberry vodka, 4 dashes of white crème de menthe, and 2.5 ounces of cranberry juice. On a plate, I crushed up a few candy canes, wet the outside rims of two chilled martini glasses by rotating the rims in simple syrup, then coated the rims with the crushed candy. I poured in the mixture and garnished the drinks with small candy canes.

"You know, you really are a talented mixologist," said Renata.

"Thank you. Four years of college and eight years of police work really came in handy," I said sarcastically. "Actually I really do love this job. It is well-suited for me. You know, I used to have anger issues once upon a time. These days I rarely ever get upset about anything. I feel like a whole different person," I said.

"Well, how about that?" said Willy. "You have finally found your calling. Maybe now you can move up a level in Maslow's hierarchy," he said with a laugh.

"Maybe," I said.

"What?" asked Renata.

"Oh, nothing," I said, giving Willy a wink and a nod. "Just an inside joke between the two of us."

About thirty minutes later, Slash arrived.

"Well, how is it going with Eileen? Is she a keeper?" I asked.

"Maybe. We'll see. I like her, but no sparks just yet."

"You are so picky," said Renata.

"Says the unmarried forty-year-old defense attorney who hasn't had a date in over a year? Hmm, want to try that again? That's the pot calling the kettle black."

"Touché," said Renata.

"What can I get for you tonight?" I asked.

"I want to try what they are drinking," he said.

"Coming right up. Now that you are all here, I need to tell you something. I have a stalker. No need to be alarmed just yet, but someone broke into my condo a few nights ago and left a cryptic message. I must have really pissed someone off recently."

"What? Holy shit. What did the note say?" asked Willy. I could almost hear all the questions shooting off in Willy's investigative journalist brain.

"The note said something about revenge, and it's sweet and served cold or something like that. As a kicker, the largest knife in my knife block was stabbed in a Christmas cake the stalker left behind."

"A cake, a note, and a knife?" said Willy. "Intriguing."

"No, not intriguing, Willy," said Slash, turning from Willy to me. "This is scary, and you should report it to the police."

"There is not really much to report. In my old line of work, I could have pissed off many people. It could literally be one of many perps."

Renata chimed in. "Actually, Selena, you should report it. This type of behavior is significantly disturbing; it does not seem like a prank. Believe me, I see all kinds of criminals, and this does not seem like a joke to me. Someone may really have it out for you. They went out of their way to craft a cryptic message and broke into your apartment. Please promise me you will report this soon."

"Okay, okay, I promise," I assured them.

"Selena, show us a card trick," said Slash, trying to change the subject. It was obvious I was a bit shaken up by the whole thing.

"Alright." I pulled out my deck of cards, and I placed a small wrapped present beside the deck of cards. I handed the cards to Slash. "Okay, Slash, you can chat with Willy and Renata and pick a card."

Renata took the deck and pulled out the joker. "This should be fun," she said.

"Good pick," said Willy.

Renata handed me the joker. I folded it in half, then folded the card in half once again. I put the card in the palm of my left hand and waved it over the small wrapped box. "Open it," I said.

Slash took the box, tore apart the wrapping paper, opened the lid, and inside the box was a folded card. Slash opened the folds, and sure enough—it was the joker.

"Holy shit. How did you do that?" said Willy.

"Magic," I said.

"I'll have to ask your nephew, Patrick. He seems to know all the tricks," said Slash.

"Okay, my turn for a dirty joke," said Willy. "I'll keep with the Christmas theme, and if you don't mind, I have a few."

"Okay," I said.

"A little boy sat on Santa's lap and said, 'Santa, all I want for Christmas is a baby brother.' Santa replies, 'That sounds great. Introduce me to your mom.'"

"Very funny," said Renata.

"I have more," said Willy excitedly. "What do snowmen use to make snow babies?"

"I don't know. What?" I asked.

"Snowballs."

"Very clever," said Renata.

"What do three ho's get you?"

"Hmm," said Slash.

"One very jolly Santa," said Willy. "One more. One more."

"Okay," I said. "But you are going to have to step up your game. Those were a bit lame."

"Why is Santa's sack so big?"

"Oh, I know this one," said Slash. "Because he only comes once a year. Christmas is so stupid. Whoever invented it should be nailed to the cross."

"Great rebuttal," said Willy. "That's hilarious."

At 9:00 p.m. some of the wedding Santas arrived. I served them the candy cane martinis, along with a few eggnog-inspired cocktails. I loved the Santa-themed wedding. The outfits were inspirational, everyone with a different take on the infamous character. One man was dressed as the Grinch version of Santa, another in a pimped-out, pinstriped Santa suit with a girl under each arm in Santa skirts and shirts that read "Santa's HO." There was a surfer Santa, who was wearing a shirt with surfing Santas and red surfer shorts, and my favorite, a jailhouse Santa wearing an orange Department of Corrections jumpsuit, a Santa hat, a white beard, and holding an empty bottle of whisky.

It was not long before Slash caught the eye of one of Santa's ho's. No judgement, it's just a costume, I thought. I am sure she is a lovely lady. Slash said to the girl, "Hey, if an old fat man puts you in a bag tonight, don't worry. I told Santa I wanted you for Christmas." Again, I was amazed that women are amused by such terrible pickup lines, but Slash sure does have a knack with the ladies.

She asked Slash, "So what do you do for a living?"

"I teach music to college kids at Florida Atlantic University in Boca."

"How interesting," she said.

"What do you do?" asked Slash.

"I am also a teacher," she said. Slash began singing the 1984 song "Hot for Teacher" by Van Halen.

"Whoa! Got it bad, got it bad, got it bad I'm hot for teacher"

At 11:00 p.m., as the speakeasy started to settle down, Lila came running toward the bar, visibly upset and crying, from the back bookcase/entrance door where Salami sat.

"Lila, what's wrong?" asked Slash.

"It's Mr. Lee. He's dead."

Chapter Twenty-Seven

Her

When Zander broke the news to Leslie about the untimely death of Mr. Lee, she did not seem shocked by the announcement. Rather, her face lit up like a child on Christmas morning. She was delighted by this revelation. He informed her that the real estate attorneys called to advise her that since Mr. Lee was dead, she would retain her position at the hotel and could continue to live in the owner's suite.

"Great news," she said.

"Great because he's dead or that you can stay on as the managing partner?"

"Both, of course. My foster mother would always tell us kids that no one is really looking out for us, and we have to create our own luck," she said. "But this is a downright Christmas miracle, Zander. We have got to celebrate."

"What would you like to do?"

"Paris. Let's spend the New Year in Paris," she said with elation. "We can ring in the New Year triumphantly, like the French would say: *Je vis ma meilleure vie*, living my best life."

"Alright then, I will make the arrangements."

Chapter Twenty-Eight

Selena & The Caretaker

Still reeling from the news about Mr. Lee's death and Lila's anguish, I was beginning to feel a little dizzy. Once everyone left the bar for the evening, I had to sit down for a moment to collect my thoughts before cleaning up. Since I'd started working here, Leslie had received a bomb threat, I was being stalked, Mr. Lee was dead, and I had been informed by Willy that at least two employees he knows of have disappeared. And, oh yeah, my sister was involved in uncovering the murderer of the former general manager's wife, who plunged from an eighth-floor balcony a few years back. There sure does seem to be a lot of death and mayhem associated with this hotel, its staff, and its patrons. Could this be a coincidence? My background as a police officer taught me that there are no coincidences.

I reached for my purse behind the bar and pulled out my cell phone. I googled "hotel deaths." What I found was astounding. There are nearly eighteen million hotel rooms across the globe, and while an estimated eighty thousand people die in a hotel room each year, the ways in which they die vary greatly. It turns out most deaths are due to suicide by the lonely, because they can be sure someone will find their body. Then there are the suicides in casino hotels like Las Vegas, where gamblers go broke or people want to have their last few nights of really feeling alive in a large luxurious hotel suite with room service and exquisite meals before either jumping from a balcony or taking pills. You won't hear about these deaths on the daily newscast because the hotel owners and the police like to keep these deaths under wraps, as it may glorify a horrific event.

The next most popular way people die in a hotel is heart attack by sex. Hotels are an aphrodisiac for some, and too much sex can kill you, apparently.

Then there is murder: stabbings, gunshot wounds, strangulation, or beatings from a vengeful adversary or a jilted lover.

Last is natural causes, of course, by elderly guests on vacation, because what else is there to do but travel when you are retired?

I read a snippet about a man who cut off his own penis—that is some crazy-ass shit. He must have taken some bad psychedelics.

I also learned that some people utilize hotels for hospice, as a beautiful place to spend their final days and be doted on by maids, room service attendants, and visiting family members.

The lights flickered, and suddenly I got a sinking feeling that I was being watched. Little hairs on the back of my neck stood on end, and tiny chills crawled up both arms. Suddenly it felt cold in the bar.

"Hello, my dear," said Hubert.

I whirled my head quickly to my right and jumped off my barstool as Hubert approached me. "Shit, you scared me! Don't sneak up on me like that!"

"You are quite jumpy these days," he said as he walked around the bar. "Can I make you a drink?"

"No, thank you," I said. "I still need to clean up before I head home."

"I will clean up for you," he offered.

"Well, alright then, sure," I said. "You can make me a Maker's Mark, neat."

"That's a stiff drink. Difficult night?"

"You could say that. One of my regular patrons, and expected part-owner of the hotel, Mr. Lee died tonight. His girlfriend, who is also one of my regular customers, was very upset about it, and trying to calm her was—well—very sad and exhausting. She said she thinks Mr. Lee was poisoned. I also have a stalker threatening me, so I am in no rush to go home right now."

"I see. There is a lot going on." Hubert glided around the bar easily, knowing where everything was located as if this was his home. He prepared my drink, planted it in the center of a purple cocktail napkin, and said, "Relax, my dear."

It dawned on me then that I couldn't remember the last time someone made *me* a drink. It felt nice to have someone to talk to, but I didn't tell Hubert this. I sat quietly for awhile as Hubert cleaned the bar for me, until Hubert finally broke the silence.

"Selena, I just want to say that I think you are doing a great job here at the Opulence Resort, and the owners are very happy with your performance."

"How would you, or they, even know that?"

"We pay attention to everything that goes on around here. I know you like secrets, so here is one for you. When you were hired here, you were told that there are cameras all over the hotel except for the speakeasy, because our esteemed customers demand privacy, but this simply is not true. We have many cameras in here, well hidden and for safety reasons mostly. We take care of our own here, and I can assure you that when you are here, you are family, and you are perfectly safe."

I was looking directly in his eyes at that moment, and I truly felt cared for, the way a child feels when their mom hugs them and tells them that everything is going to be okay. I could feel a small tear fall and burn my cheek, and a rush of emotion fueled more tears. Now I felt like a blubbering idiot. I was not exactly sure why I was crying, but I think it was just everything that had happened to me over the past few months. Killing a perp, losing my job, being stalked and afraid to go home, and the death of Mr. Lee, whom I hardly knew. It was just a lot to take in. Climbing down an internet rabbit hole of hotel deaths did not help either. I should have been stronger, but I let the tears flow, because I know from experience that after a good cry, I would feel much better.

"Excuse me," I said softly. "I am going to go to the restroom to clean myself up."

When I returned, Hubert was gone. But I saw movement. The coffee table and the rug beneath it, centered between the couches in the lounge area, glided toward me, stopped abruptly, then moved back to its original location. "Holy frigging Hogwarts!" I said out loud for no one to hear. Now I know your hiding place, I thought. An entrance to a cellar maybe or storage space hidden under the coffee table. I will pin that thought for now. I am too exhausted, and I need to get some sleep.

Chapter Twenty-Nine

Her

Zander made the arrangements to travel to Paris over the New Year holiday. He hoped to convince Leslie not to return to the States. She had enough money to travel the world over and still have plenty of money left before settling on a permanent place to reside. He worried that too many deaths had followed her, and soon the police might be suspicious. Her first husband died of a stroke, her second a heart attack, and now Mr. Lee was presumed poisoned right before a corporate takeover which would remove her from the residence and managing partnership. In a world filled with insane conspiracy theories, all it would take was one nosy journalist or detective suggesting she had a motive for murder to make their lives miserable.

"I want to attend the hotel Christmas party on the twenty-third," said Leslie. "I know we have to leave early the following day for our trip, but it would be nice to wish everyone a Merry Christmas before we take off for France."

"Geez, since when are you so sentimental?" said Zander.

"I am not really, but I am quite fond of all the regulars in the speakeasy. Selena and even her difficult sister Talia have grown on me over these past few months."

"You are getting soft, Leslie."

"Maybe it's just a smidge of Christmas joy."

Chapter Thirty

Selena

When I awoke, I was still exhausted. Then I heard Robert De Niro speak to me in my head: You'll have time to rest when you are dead.

Dead. That worries me. Then I remembered the security company was scheduled to come by this morning to install a deadbolt lock on my front door, window locks, and cameras at the entrance and back slider of the balcony. An app on my phone will monitor any activity and alert me if it detects movement while I am away. I was thankful that the condo agreed to install these security measures and make these arrangements for me.

By 3:00 p.m., when the installation was complete, I started to settle down a bit and felt a little less anxious. I am going to be just fine, I said to myself over and over again until I began to believe it. When I pulled out my checkbook to pay the security technician, he informed me that he had already been paid. That is strange, I thought.

Did the condo pay for all this security? It seemed dubious, so I made a mental note to get to the bottom of that later. I needed to get ready for work.

At 3:30 p.m., while walking to work, I stopped by the park to visit with Jenny. I peeked in the gazebo, but she was not there, and all I found was her shopping bag, filled with her belongings, and her cat, who looked very hungry.

"Hey, you," said an old homeless man watching me from the park bench.

"Yes," I said, "I was just dropping by to check on Jenny."

"She is not here," he said. "Last night she trailed off to follow a teenager, and I never saw her again."

"Oh no. What did the teenager look like?"

"I don't know . . . young, thin—could have been a teenage girl or boy. I couldn't really tell."

"I need to get to work, but I am going to call 911. Please meet with the police when they get here, and take the cat food out of her shopping bag and feed kitty, please."

"Okay, I will," he said.

I hoped that Jenny was alright, and I wondered if the police would even care that a homeless lady had gone missing. I presume that the police would not take this disappearance seriously, but I called 911 and reported the incident nevertheless. The dispatcher said they would send a police officer to the park later to investigate.

When I got to work, Hubert met me at the entrance of the speakeasy. "I heard Smith Security installed hardware at your condo today."

"Yes, sir. How did you know that? It happened just a few hours ago."

"I told you, you are family now. We take care of our own, and I was worried about you and the stalker you spoke of last night."

"Was it you that paid for the security at my condo?" I asked.

"The management and owners take care of their own," he said with a wide smile. "You will be safe now."

"Thank you," I said, and I went to hug him, but he moved away, holding out his right hand as if to say stop. He said, "No need."

I nodded, walked behind the bar, and when I turned around to thank him once again, he was gone.

Today Lila was the first to arrive. "Hello, Selena. I am so sorry to have alarmed everyone yesterday, but I was really distraught. I just completed my interview at the police station."

"How did that go?" I asked.

"A little scary at first, but the officers were very caring."

"Do they have any idea who could have done this?"

"No idea, but James, Mr. Lee's assistant, said that he thinks it was Leslie. He said only Leslie would have a motive to do this, and the police are looking into the courier that delivered the fatal tea."

"This is so devastating," I said.

"James gave me this," she said. Lila opened a light-blue Tiffany box, and inside was a beautiful engagement ring, the diamond sparkling brilliantly despite the morbid circumstances. "He was going to propose to me."

"I am so sorry, Lila," I said sadly.

"James suggested that I sell the ring to pay off my debts for medical school. I am not sure that I have the heart to do that though. The ring is so beautiful, and it's a reminder of the life we could have shared together."

"I understand. It is so very unsettling. Can I at least offer you a drink to help calm your nerves?"

"Yes, please. A French 75."

"Coming right up."

Patrick was the next to arrive.

"How did you get in here?" I asked sternly.

"The same way you come in, behind the front desk, down the stairs, and then I use this key." He pulled out a key from his right pocket.

"Patrick," I said, "where did you steal that?"

"I snatched it from the concierge desk. They really need to be more careful where they lay their keys. Thieves are everywhere."

"Ugh, Patrick, you are going to give your mom a heart attack. She will be very angry if she finds out," I said.

"Well, that is why you are not going to tell her," he said with the biggest grin he could muster and folded his hands as if to pray. "Please?"

"You are lucky you're cute," I said reluctantly. "We'll talk more about this later. Do you want a Shirley Temple?"

"Sure, with a splash of Bacardi, please," he said.

"You are pushing your luck, Patrick."

"Okay, Aunt Selena, I'll be good."

"You are adorable," said Lila

"I am not adorable. I'm ten. Babies are adorable."

"Sorry, did I say adorable?" Lila corrected herself. "I meant to say smart and handsome."

"Much better, thank you." He blushed.

"Are you the lady who was dating Mr. Lee?"

"Yes," Lila said. "How did you know that?"

"I heard the bellmen talking about it."

"What did the bellmen say exactly?"

"Well, they think Leslie—well, they called her the black widow. They think she may have something to do with it, and so does my mom. Seems too easy to assume Leslie did it. It's too obvious, and I am sorry for your loss," said Patrick.

"Thank you," said Lila. "If the police show up here, you should tell them what you heard."

"No way. My mom would never let me talk to cops, but I will listen in and report back to you though. Can I have your phone number?"

"My boyfriend just died. It is going to be a while before I hand out my phone number again. This kid, Selena," said Lila.

I completed her sentence: "I know, I know. He sure is something else."

"I am right here, you know. I can hear you," said Patrick.

Old man Wilcox and Slash arrived next. "Oh no, the menace is here. I'll sit over here by Lila to make sure that thief doesn't steal my money or watch today," said Slash. Lila got up to hug both Willy and Slash.

"We are so sorry for all that you are going through right now," said Willy.

"Please let us know if there is anything we can do," said Slash.

"You are doing it. Just being here for me right now," said Lila.

"Where is Renata today?" I asked.

"Working on a case. I don't think we will see her for a few days," said Slash. "I am sure she will be here for the hotel Christmas party. It's the party of the year, you know. Free drinks for the regulars and gifts from the general manager, so tell Talia not to be cheap this year."

"You got it," I said.

"Alright, Selena. A card trick, please," said Willy.

"Nope, not today. Patrick will ruin the trick."

"Then maybe Patrick can show us a trick," said Willy.

"Can I?" asked Patrick. "Please, Aunt Selena?"

"Okay, go ahead. Here is the deck of cards."

"Nope. I have my own deck of cards," he said.

Patrick took a deck of cards from his jacket pocket. He laid them all out on the bar counter for everyone to see. He asked everyone to pick a card, a different card for everyone, don't touch it, just think about it. Willy, Lila, and I all chose a card but did not say the card out loud. Patrick shuffled the deck, then picked three cards from the deck and placed a card in front of each of us. He said, "Is this the card you chose?"

We each said, "No," "No," and "No."

"Of course it is not, because card tricks aren't real, and magic is stupid."

"Very funny, Patrick," I said. "When is your mom picking you up?"

"Soonish," he said.

Thirty minutes later, Talia arrived and said, "Patrick, I am sorry I am late. My meeting with the owners just ended. Thank you, Selena, for watching him. He was supposed to stay with Peter in concierge," Talia said, with a vicious side-eye and a small smack in the back of his head. "But it doesn't surprise me to find him here."

"No problem. He is a real joy," Slash said sarcastically.

"Let's go, Patrick," said Talia.

"Alright," said Patrick. "Just one more thing." Patrick held his deck of cards, pulled out three cards, and handed one to each of us, which happened to be the cards we had chosen in our minds. "Here," he said. "My gift to you."

"Holy shit—that kid is gifted," said Slash.

"Patrick," said Talia, "give Slash his watch back."

Chapter Thirty-One

Her

About twenty minutes before closing, Leslie entered the speakeasy. By that time, everyone had gone home for the evening.

"Hi, Leslie," said Selena.

"I could really go for a glass of Bordeaux. Would you mind if I sit here while you clean up?" she asked.

"Of course not. My pleasure. The death of Mr. Lee has everyone talking around here. How are you holding up?"

"Not so well. I spoke with the police today. I told them that I did not send Mr. Lee the Korean tea, but I don't think they believed me. They are presuming he was poisoned, but toxicology will take a few weeks. I had to get special permission to vacation to France for the New Year."

"Will you be attending the Christmas party on the twenty-third?"

"Yes, I wouldn't miss it," Leslie said. "We leave for Paris the next day, but I hear the hotel's annual Christmas party is a blast."

"What do *you* think happened to Mr. Lee?" asked Selena.

"No idea. His death, however, keeps me on as managing partner, which makes me a suspect. But my ownership stays the same whether or not I am the managing director, so why would I kill someone for a stupid job?"

"Good question. I hope you expressed that fact to the police," Selena said.

"I did. I think that is why they are allowing me to leave the country."

"Well, if it is any consolation, I wholeheartedly believe you are innocent."

"Thank you, Selena," she said. "But truth be told, we haven't known each other for long. What makes you so sure?"

"A gifted bartender has the ability to look past what other people want you to see. I see you, Leslie. You are no murderer."

"Thank you for that," she said sincerely. Tiny tears escaped from her sad eyes that Selena pretended not to see.

Chapter Thirty-Two

Selena

I walked home that evening hoping to see Jenny, hoping against all hope that she had returned. Instead I found the old man in the gazebo tonight, sleeping with her cat. I didn't disturb him from his slumber. I left a small white bag from Five Guys, filled with a bacon cheeseburger and french fries, for him by his pillow.

I was frightened for Jenny. She had warned me about someone following me, and now I must return the favor to find out what happened to her. I made a mental note to call the police station in the morning to follow up on the report that was made and see if there were any leads as to where she may be. She would never leave her cat behind, and I had a sinking feeling that I may never see Jenny again.

Chapter Thirty-Three

Selena

The police had no leads as to the whereabouts of Jenny. My condo had no further attempted break-ins or any activity at all. I called my sister to check in and work through a few questions I wanted to ask but hadn't had the chance to chat with her about. The hotel had been so busy lately. I picked up my cell phone and called Talia.

"Hello, Selena," she said. "Please tell me you are alright."

"I'm fine," I said.

"So, what's up?"

"I just wanted to say thank you for paying for the security at my condo."

"What security?"

"Hubert told me that the hotel picked up the cost of my home security system after my break-in."

"Selena, are you feeling okay?"

"What do you mean?"

"I am lost here. Back up. What security system?"

"After my break-in, I installed a home security system, but when I pulled out my checkbook to pay, I was told that it was already paid for. When I got to work later that day, Hubert said that hotel management and the owners paid for it because they wanted to keep me safe."

"Selena, who is Hubert?"

"You know, the caretaker of the speakeasy. He comes around pretty often. I met him on my first day. He gave me the grand tour of the hotel."

"Selena, we don't have a caretaker."

Chapter Thirty-Four

Selena & The Christmas Party

The big day had arrived. The day everyone was so excited for. The hotel Christmas party would commence in the speakeasy. I expected about two hundred hotel staffers for the cocktail hour and all of the local patrons to be in attendance. The guests would later escape to the grand ballroom and return for an aperitif and visit from Santa, the man himself.

Today when I finished setting up my bar, I couldn't help but stare at the coffee table, rug, and marble tiles beneath it. I could not distract my thoughts about who may be working or residing under the floor tiles. Talia said that there is no Hubert. If there is no Hubert, who have I been talking to all these months? I have no special abilities and have never conversed with ghosts. There had to be a more reasonable explanation. One of the last times we met, Hubert's disappearing Houdini act ended with a glimpse of movement from the coffee table. I walked cautiously over to the lounge area, almost in a tiptoe, which is silly. What could happen? No one was going to jump out at me. My mind was whirling with possibilities. Will the coffee table move on its own? Is there a remote hidden somewhere that will open the secret entrance? Just as I got close to the table, I heard someone call my name.

"Hey, pretty lady," yelled old man Wilcox.

"Jesus Christ!" I exclaimed while metaphorically jumping out of my skin. "You scared me. You are here early today; we don't open for another fifteen minutes," I said, flustered, heart racing, my cheeks hot, like I had been caught with my hands in the cookie jar. "I wasn't expecting anyone just yet," I said. Now I was going to have to investigate what or who was beneath the lounge floor another time.

"I am sorry. Just excited about tonight," he said with a smile.

"You look very nice tonight. You shaved off your mustache and beard. I hardly recognized you, and I love the Santa tie. Can I get you a drink or would you like to try my specialty drink for this evening?"

"The specialty drink. I am feeling festive tonight."

"Coming right up, a sugar cookie martini."

In a shaker, I added ice, 1 ounce of vanilla vodka, 1 ounce of amaretto, a splash of whole milk, and a splash of Baileys. I poured the mixture into a martini glass that I rimmed with vanilla frosting and multi-colored sprinkles. I garnished it with a sugar cookie from a batch of cookies the pastry chef had dropped off just a few minutes ago. "The sugar cookie is straight from the oven, compliments of Chef Kate."

"I am ever impressed with your cocktail creations. This is pretty fantastic, almost too pretty to drink. You really need to add your specialty drinks to the bartender's bible."

"Thank you," I said. "I'm going to make a large batch for the cocktail hour this evening, and yes, that's a great idea. I *will* add my specialty drink recipes to the bartender's bible, which will forever place them within the speakeasy's extraordinary history for a future bartender and his patrons to enjoy."

By 5:00 p.m. Renata had arrived. "Holy shit," said Willy. "You clean up nicely."

"Thank you, Willy. I can't remember the last time I wore a cocktail dress. I spent too much time in the courtroom this year. I am going to make a resolution to get out more often next year," she said. "You look pretty dapper yourself. I like the freshly shaved look. You look ten years younger."

"Thank you for the compliment. I feel great tonight, and I have some advice for you. Life is short, Renata. Believe me, I've got one foot in the grave already," said Willy. "Don't spend so much time on your career. Life will pass you by. What is it that people say? No one on their deathbed says, 'I should have spent more time at work.'"

"True. I promise to heed your advice, dear friend," she said.

Lila and Slash arrived next, together, arm in arm. "Hello, you two. You both look lovely this fine evening," I said. I was impressed Slash had retired his leather jacket for a black suit and a tie with dancing snowmen. Lila looked stunning in a long red sequin gown that appeared specifically tailored for her tall and slender figure. Slash positioned himself right under the mistletoe

I'd hung earlier in the evening. He looked up at it and sang:

> *"I should be playing in the winter snow*
> *But I'ma be under the mistletoe*
> *With you, shawty with you"*

"Hey, that is not an eighties song. That's Justin Bieber," Renata said, looking puzzled.

"Yeah, I have to admit I am a big fan. Promise not to tell anyone."

"I am so glad every one of you made it here tonight for the party. I made specialty cocktails." I served Slash and Lila and said, "Merry Christmas and enjoy."

If I were to rate my happiness level on a scale of ten in that moment, I would say that it was a nine. I never thought that my life and career path would usher me to a place where I would make such great friends and experience such joy. Not a ten, however, because I couldn't escape the mystery behind Hubert, my stalker, Jenny's whereabouts, and Mr. Lee's tragic death. But I put those thoughts aside for the moment and tried my best to enjoy the night's festivities.

The next to arrive was Talia and her date, Patrick. "Hey, little man. You look splendid this evening," I said.

"Thank you, Aunt Selena," he said. "I'll have a Manhattan on the rocks."

"You most certainly will not," said Talia.

"Mom, you are such a buzzkill," said Patrick.

"What am I gonna do with this kid?" asked Talia facetiously with a shrug.

"I know what I am going to do. I am putting my watch in my pocket," said Slash.

"It's not safe there either," said Patrick gleefully.

The last to arrive before the hotel staffers were Leslie and Zander.

"Hello, Selena. Hello, Talia," said Zander.

"Hello," I said. Talia looked away, pretending she did not hear him.

"Merry Christmas, Selena," said Leslie. "Zander and I are leaving in the morning for Paris, and I wanted to make sure I wished you happy holidays."

"Here is a gift for you from the two of us—well, mostly me," she said.

I opened the gift immediately. I had not expected a gift from anyone, let alone

Leslie, but I presumed she felt we had bonded over these past few months. I don't think she has many friends, or any at all really, and I was grateful for the sentiment. A small box with gold wrapping paper and a matching bow beautifully concealed a necklace of white gold, with a martini glass pendant embellished with miniature diamonds. "This is just gorgeous. Thank you. I am going to put it on right now."

Zander rushed behind the bar to help me place it on my neck. He made my neck hair stand on end. I always felt a bit creeped out in his company. My sister was off her barstool, just waiting to pounce should he try any funny business. I glanced at Talia and gave her a nod to let her know not to worry, that I could take care of myself.

"Thank you for being a friend to me this past year when no one else would," Leslie said sincerely. "I truly appreciate it and have greatly enjoyed your company. Do you believe that you meet certain people in your life, at a specific time, for a reason? I feel like you and I were meant to meet, maybe even influence the course of my life. I know that is really heavy for a Christmas party, but that is how I feel."

"Yes, that is the premise behind *The Celestine Prophecy* by James Redfield. People come into your life at a certain time to teach you something that will influence your future and life's purpose."

"Upon my return, we will have to discuss your future here at the Opulence Resort. I would love to offer you an executive management position here. We can of course discuss all of the details in the new year."

"Oh my, thank you. I am very thankful for this job, and I really love working here." Suddenly I felt like my happiness level reached a nine point five. I can't say that I had ever really felt like I made a real impact on anyone's life in a positive way.

"One more thing," said Leslie. "I have something special for Willy. Here you go old man." Leslie handed a small, gift wrapped package to Willy, as his eyes twinkled with excitement."

"This is for me? Really? Thank you," said Willy joyfully. He opened the package with reckless abandon, then suddenly looked baffled. Inside the box were three Energizer AAA batteries and a note. It read:

Gift not included.
-Love Leslie

I had never seen Willy laugh so hard, and all at once, we chimed in with laughter of our own.

"Not to break up the lovefest," said Talia, "but where is Salami tonight? Shouldn't he be here already?"

"Salami is here," I said. "The company that was supposed to send Santa tonight called earlier to tell us Santa had a scheduling conflict, so Salami volunteered to step in. He went home to collect his Santa suit and should return soon."

"He just so happened to have a Santa suit at home?" asked Slash.

"I guess so," I said.

"This evening better go smoothly," said Talia. "I don't like having so many people in the speakeasy tonight without someone manning the back door or regulating the crowd."

"I am sure we will be fine," said Leslie. "Tonight it's just us staffers and regular patrons. We should be safe, and he should be here soon."

"The Salami I know will have an eye on the back door and a hand on his revolver, even in Santa attire," said Willy.

"The revolver better be well hidden. A gun-toting Santa is not a good look for the hotel," said Talia.

"Mom, can I sit on Santa's lap?" asked Patrick.

"Why? No, Patrick—you cannot steal Santa's gun."

"Mom, I wasn't—"

"No, Patrick," said Talia.

At a few minutes before 6:00 p.m., I received a phone call from Peter in concierge. "People will begin arriving for the Christmas party in about thirty minutes," he said. "You can open the speakeasy doors then."

"Alright, I will be ready. Let me replenish everyone's drinks so the staffers can have my complete attention. Call me back in thirty."

As I was filling up everyone's martini glasses with the sugar cookie martini batch I had prepared, and Talia was gifting iPads to all of the regulars as a special gift on behalf of the Opulence Resort, I heard a loud pop. There, standing in the doorway of the speakeasy and holding a Smith & Wesson toward the ceiling, was a familiar face. A face that haunted my dreams. It was Jade, that poor beaten and broken girl I left alone and afraid on my last day on the job. What was she doing here, dressed like a ninja and wielding a firearm?

"Jade?" I said. "Is that you?" I tried to remain calm as everyone at the bar fell to the floor by instinct.

"Don't anyone move," yelled Jade. "No one needs to get hurt except for that bitch behind the bar."

"What? I am confused. I saved your life."

"Saved my life? No, you *did not* save my life. You killed my boyfriend, the only man, or person, that ever loved me. You killed him and left me there, never once checking up on me to see how I was doing. I was alone with no one to help me. I had no money, no place to live, and a drug addiction I could no longer afford. You deserve to pay for killing him."

"Okay, okay," said Zander as he stood up from the lounge floor. "How about you put the gun down, then you and Selena can talk about this calmly while I make you a drink. How about that?"

"Selena, you sit over here," Jade said as she pulled a barstool to the center of the floor. "The rest of you stay put." Jade pointed the gun back and forth from me to everyone else sitting on the marble floor.

I walked from behind the bar to the barstool she demanded I sit on, while Zander said to Leslie, "I've got this. She just wants attention. I am sure she means no harm to anyone here." Leslie nodded in agreement. Zander said to Jade, "I am going to make you a drink to settle your nerves, and then we can talk about this. No one needs to get hurt."

"Okay," she said. "Make me something fancy."

Zander slowly and carefully walked behind the bar with his hands above his head. He crafted one of the speakeasy's signature drinks, the key lime martini, but before completion, he retrieved the Gatorade bottle from the refrigerator, which he'd left there a few weeks ago under the premise that the bottle contained a sugary drink to offset a diabetic crash from the diabetes he did not have. He poured in a generous amount of the green liquid, then shook and poured the concoction into a crystal Mikasa martini glass and garnished it with a key lime wheel and a touch of whipped cream. He centered it gingerly on top of a square purple cocktail napkin with a generous smile. "Come, sit and have a drink with us," he said.

From the rear entrance, Salami appeared in Santa attire, yelling, "HO HO HO!" This must have startled Jade because she shot at him twice. The second bullet landed in his right shoulder, and he fell to the floor. Without thinking, Lila ran to his aid. While Lila was in motion, Salami reached for his gun with his uninjured arm.

"No!" screamed Zander. "No!" Salami moved his arm back to the floor, and Zander said, "Come, Jade, sit down, and let's talk about this."

All of this commotion created a distraction for Patrick to peel away from Talia's arms, and he raced behind the bar to press a button that alerted security. Holding the button down, he said, "I need an old-fashioned with extra cherries," and scurried back to his mother's arms.

Jade just stood stoically in shock, expressionless, her face showing no remorse for shooting Salami. She turned to me next, pointing her gun in my face, and said, "Not only did you kill my boyfriend, you made me kill that poor homeless lady. She followed me, and then I had to kill her and dump her body under the boardwalk. I did not want to do that. I just wanted to kill *you*."

"You killed that poor homeless woman for nothing. She was harmless. I killed your boyfriend by accident. He hit you, so I hit him, protecting you. I had no intention of killing him. I am haunted by that every day. It was you who left me the cake and message about revenge wasn't it?"

"You said you would call me," said Jade, "keep in touch with me, but you just killed my boyfriend and walked away like I never mattered."

"I meant to call you. I did. But when I was fired, I was advised to leave the job behind. Which meant I could not contact anyone I dealt with in a professional capacity any longer since I was no longer a police officer."

"You uncaring bitch. I should just shoot you right here," she said as she walked over to the bar. She sat on the stool, still pointing her gun back and forth between Zander, me, Salami, and everyone else cowering on the floor. Talia squeezed Patrick, keeping him close. Willy looked down at the floor, trying not to make eye contact. Slash was watching Lila. Renata had her phone hidden behind her back, recording the entire encounter. Leslie was immobile, paralyzed in fear.

Zander stole Salami and Lila's attention for a moment by waving his hands above his head in their direction. He nodded his head and said, "I got this. Stand down." It was no wonder even someone as tiny as Jade was not intimidated by Zander. He stood there, five feet, six inches tall, skin sweaty, with a sheepish grin like a nerdy bookworm trying to make a friend. The phone rang, and I was sure that it was probably Peter from concierge trying to tell me that it was time to open the speakeasy door.

"Don't answer the phone," said Jade.

"I am going to have to answer the phone soon, or the party guests are going to get worried and call security," I said.

"Give me a minute and let me think," she said. She raised her martini glass—a gesture to the ladies, bartender, and patrons to acknowledge and greet them, as if to say, "Cheers." She took a small sip, licked her lips, and declared to her captive audience, "Vengeance never tasted so sweet." She then took two large gulps and, with her tongue, finished off the graham cracker rim and smiled a wide, indulgent grin.

Thirty seconds later, she slumped slightly over the bar, holding her midsection, then suddenly fainted, falling sideways off the barstool. She thrashed around on the floor, mouth foaming with lime green bubbling saliva. Her fingers curled, blood trickled from her nose and ears, and her right foot shook uncontrollably, releasing her loose-laced red plaid Jeffrey Campbell high-heeled boot from her writhing body.

The ladies watched, but did not budge to help her in any way. Instead, the ladies formed a circle around her, exhibiting no immediate signs of shock. Faces expressionless, the horror mirrored in each other's eyes eventually gave in to twisted smiles and an eerie sense of glee.

After approximately three silent minutes, Jade stopped all movement as her eyelids slowly crept open. Still, no one spoke a word. The ladies and bar patrons just leered maliciously at the woman's lifeless body on the cold marble floor.

Zander waited approximately fifteen minutes before making the obligatory call to both hotel security and 911.

Before opening the door of the speakeasy, Leslie said, "Zander, what did you put in her drink?"

"A propriety blend of ingredients including a generous amount of methyl iodide, undetectable in a toxicology report, but in a nutshell, the solution mimics a stroke or seizure."

"Please, Zander, tell me that you did not kill Mr. Lee in the same manner," pleaded Leslie. "My two former husbands? What about them?"

"Leslie, ever since we were kids, it was my job to look after you. After Mom and Dad died and we were separated, I promised myself that when I found you again, I would take care of you."

"What the fuck is going on?" said Talia.

"Talia, Zander is my brother, not my husband. Because we have the same last name, everyone presumes he is my husband, but they are mistaken."

"Holy shit. What are we going to tell the cops?" said Slash.

"They are already on their way," said Patrick. "I called in the safety word."

"Thank God Patrick pays attention to everything around here," said Talia.

Everyone was silent for a few moments. I detected movement from the lounge. The coffee table moved toward me, and Hubert emerged from below. "Thank God you are here," said Salami.

"How badly are you injured?" asked Hubert.

"I am fine. She just grazed my shoulder."

"Perfect," said Hubert. He opened the bookcase entrance so it stayed open to the parking lot. He picked Jade up from the floor and threw her body over his left shoulder. She looked tiny on the shoulder of his nearly seven-foot frame. "I will take care of her body. You will tell the police the entire truth up to when she drank the cocktail. You will tell the police that she ran out the back door after the phone rang. Tell them she was afraid partygoers would soon arrive, so she left. No body, no crime. We take care of our own here at the Opulence Resort. Someone, please clean the floor. She left a mess." Renata stopped the recording on her phone, but instead of saving it, she deleted it. Hubert looked at Renata and said, "Good choice." Hubert then turned and disappeared beneath the floor.

"Holy shit. I knew it. I knew it," said Willy. "There *is* a secret room or vault."

"Who the fuck was that?" asked Talia.

"*That*, Sis, is Hubert, the caretaker."

"Well, thank fucking God for him."

And just like that, my happiness level fell to a one. Note to self: life is fleeting and unpredictable. Enjoy all the little moments of joy because you never know how long they will last.

When the police arrived, we repeated the story accurately up until Jade drank the key lime martini. Then, as suggested, we altered the details of her final departure. If you had asked me a week ago if there could be any circumstance at all to cause an ex-police officer, an investigative reporter, a medical resident, and a defense attorney to lie to a police officer about a murder they witnessed, I would have said no, never. Today, however, our friendship and loyalty to the Opulence Resort and each other prevailed, and the fictionalized story about a vengeful vigilante coming for justice for Selena will become memorialized in the hotel's history.

Epilogue

Selena
Two Weeks Later

A two-week vacation was much needed. The speakeasy was closed by the police for that evening as they prepared their report. Consequently, Talia closed the lounge for the remaining few weeks over the holidays so everyone could decompress and recover from the disturbing events of that evening. During that time period, I worked with the local police to find Jenny's body under the boardwalk and get ahold of her next of kin. I still whisper "Hello, Jenny" into the wind for no one to hear when I pass the gazebo, just in case she is still looking out for me.

Upon my return to work, a custom purple-and-gold embossed letter was left for me on the bar counter. I didn't need to read the return address to know that the letter was sent by Leslie from her new home in Paris. The letter read:

Dear Selena,

*A good friend, like a four-leaf clover, is hard
to find and lucky to have. A real friend
knows you well, understands where you have
been, accepts where you are, and
encourages you to become the person you
hope to be.*

I will forever cherish our friendship.

*Love,
Leslie*

Moments later, I was greeted by
Hubert. "I suppose I have some explaining
to do," he said. "I work for the owners and
their partners. My father before me and his
father before him have taken on the same
role. We are paid well to keep the Opulence
Resort safe for those who matter."

"I have heard from Willy that the
Opulence may have been involved with
murder in the past. He has been looking for
two individuals who disappeared in the
forties."

"Like I said, we take care of our own.
They did, in fact, disappear. The two were
escorted off the property one summer
evening and brought to Washington state by

one of our employees. My father was fearful for their safety, so he moved them far away for their own safety from the owners at the time."

"This place sure is full of surprises."

"Selena, it pains me to say that today will be my final day. The owners will replace me with someone I am sure will be quite capable. As a parting gift, I left the hotel journals dating back from the hotel's opening in 1920. The journals include the caretaker reports prepared every evening. Please make sure Mr. Wilcox reads these journals. He has been waiting a lifetime for his questions to be answered. Promise me that after he reads them, he will return them to the vault beneath the floor. I look forward to reading the story about this hotel's history one day. I am sure Mr. Wilcox will be inspired to write an excellent book, with special care for all of us who keep this place close to our hearts." Hubert took a deep breath and continued. "I wish I had the opportunity to say goodbye to Mr. Salamoni. Please tell him that I greatly enjoyed working with him over the years when he returns from his long-awaited trip to Sicily."

"I promise," I said. He then gave me a photograph of his grandfather standing next to his twenty-five-year-old father and a small child, which must be himself.

"This is a photo of my family. All three of us Huberts. Keeping this place safe has become my family's life's work."

I took the photo and stood it up in the middle of the bar, on the shelf with the Prohibition gin. "I will display this photo with pride," I said happily.

"Congratulations on your promotion to director of special events—a perfect job specially created just for you. You deserve it. Leslie and Zander made a wise choice to stay in Paris to keep the police's prying eyes away from their sordid past. I think we all misjudged Leslie, and I truly feel for her, having to take care of her murderous brother. No amount of money in the world can fix the problems Zander has to contend with. I hope he finds a competent psychologist. Oh, and one more thing," he said as he pulled out a small wallet. "Give this back to Patrick. I lifted it from his back pocket in the elevator earlier today."

"So it was you that encouraged his thieving ways," I said. "I did not see that one coming."

"Yes, he found me in the vault the day he arrived here. That kid is something else.

We have been friends ever since. Say congratulations to your sister as well for taking over as managing partner."

"Will do," I said, and I reached for a hug, but this time, instead of pulling away, he hugged me back, a big, satisfying bear hug that lasted just as long as we both needed it to.

Selena
Present Day

Hello, my name is Selena. You are always welcome here at the Flamingo Lounge. If you ever find yourself in Palm Beach, come for a visit.

Your secrets are safe with me.

Turn the page to enjoy a short horror story…

"Never marry the one you can live with;
marry the one you cannot live without."
—Unknown

TILL DEATH

LEAH ORR

T ruth be told, I had never intended to jump. I was just trying to make a dramatic statement.

"I would rather die than live without you," I said as I climbed onto the sill of the bridal suite window. Gripping the window pane tightly, I assured him that I would surely jump if he walked out the hotel room door.

"Do it," he said, calling my bluff.

"I will. I mean it. Please forgive me," I pleaded. "It happened just once, and I don't love him. It is only you I love. Don't walk out that door. I will jump. Please don't leave me."

He hardly looked upset when he turned around to leave me standing there on the windowsill. He made his own dramatic statement by slamming the door behind him.

I stood there in the window, crying hysterically, watching passersby below point to me in fear for my life and the devastation of what they may witness if I decided to make the leap. People are so pathetic, I thought. While some actually looked scared for me, others looked excited about the prospect of witnessing a real live jumper.

Marriage is not for everyone. Some say people are not meant to be together forever and that monogamy is a nearly impossible goal for most individuals. I did not mean to cheat on him. I swear my ex-husband, Jared, must have slipped something in my drink, a revenge of sorts for leaving him last year. I don't even have any recollection of what transpired that night other than the photos that were sent to my phone and the phones of our wedding guests.

Revenge porn is how I would label it. But no one would ever believe me, and now I don't know how to fix this problem. Couldn't he at least have waited until tomorrow to send this photo? Then I could have kept the beautiful memory of our wedding night before having to uncover the facts and explain the events of that evening.

I never should have agreed to meet with Jared last week. My friends warned me that nothing good could come of it. But I felt obligated. Although Jared and I were only married less than a year, I felt that I owed him a moment before I became someone else's wife. I met him at Christine's Bar and Grill. I remember drinking a glass of pinot grigio, and then my next memory was waking up in my own bed, wearing pajamas that were not my favorites. Trying to piece together the evening, I called Jared, but he did not answer. I left messages, but he did not return my phone calls. When I told my friends what happened, they promised to get to the bottom of it, but no one could find Jared. He was not in his apartment or any of the local hangouts, and his friends hadn't heard from him in a few days. They told me to forget about him and concentrate on the wedding. I heeded that advice, but still that evening with Jared haunted me.

It was 11:00 p.m. when the bartender called out, "Last call for alcohol." At that moment, everyone's phone received a photo text of me, half naked and asleep in my bed with Jared smiling beside me, a proud selfie for all to see. You could tell the photo was recent because you could clearly see my engagement ring on my hand draped over my stomach while I slept.

My new husband, Tommy, grabbed me in an instant, pushed me into the elevator, and forced me into the bridal suite. Tommy displayed a grand arsenal of emotions—anger, humiliation, and overwhelming sadness. I tried to explain that I had no recollection of the evening that photo was taken, but he would not listen.

"Why would you meet with Jared anyway? I thought it was over between the two of you. Why would you do this to me?" he said, painfully trying his best to hold back tears that would eventually come without permission.

After he left the suite, I tried to climb down from the sill. My heel caught in the ledge, and instead of propelling me inside, backward I tumbled, falling twelve stories, like a fallen bridal angel in the night sky onto the traffic below.

Seconds, minutes, hours passed. I cannot recollect time now that I am dead. Sadly, heaven is not where I ended up, but here I reside, back in the bridal suite. I am trapped here, with no way to escape, in my wedding gown.

These days I loom over brides and their new husbands on their wedding nights, and I delight in their joy and wonder why I am still stuck here. While I can't extract time from my new existence, I have spent time with three sets of newlyweds, so I am guessing three weekends have passed.

Today the newscaster is speaking from the television. The body of a man was found dead on the sidewalk of the Ocean Breeze Condominiums. Mr. Jared Williams was pronounced dead after falling from his seventeenth-floor balcony this evening. Authorities are not considering foul play.

I suddenly felt a cold chill and breath upon my neck, and when I looked behind me, there was Jared, smiling back at me. "When you married me, you made a commitment," he said. "Till death do us part. You broke that commitment. So I had to take drastic measures. I broke up your marriage, so you could be with me. I didn't expect you to end your life, so I had to end mine. Now In death, we shall be together forever."

Enjoy a few cocktails from:

The
Bartender's
Bible

Key Lime Martini

In a shaker with ice add:
4 ounces of vanilla vodka
3 tablespoons of condensed milk
3 1/2 tablespoons of lime juice
3 1/2 tablespoons of pineapple juice

Rim the martini glass first with corn syrup
then crushed graham crackers

Strain cocktail into the martini glass

Add a dollop of whipped cream

Garnish with a key lime wheel

Old School Dirty Martini
(Zander)

In a shaker with ice add:
2 1/2 ounces of Old London Dock gin
1/2 ounce of dry Martini & Rossi vermouth
2 dashes of Regan's orange bitters
A splash of olive juice to make it dirty

Stir slowly, then strain cocktail into a chilled martini glass

Garnish with classic green olives skewered on a toothpick

Mary Pickford
(Renata)

In a cocktail shaker with ice add:
1 1/2 ounces of Bacardi Superior rum
1 1/2 ounces of pineapple juice
1 teaspoon of grenadine
5 drops of maraschino liqueur

Shake and strain into a martini glass

Garnish with a maraschino cherry

Frozen Ginger Pear Bourbon Martini

(Slash)

In the blender with ice add:
3 ounces of Old Fitzgerald Kentucky bourbon
3 slices of a pear
A sliver of ginger
1 ounce of Cock'n Bull ginger beer
A splash of Sprite

After blending, pour into a martini glass

Sprinkle cinnamon in the center

Garnish with a slice of pear

French 75
(Lila)

In a cocktail shaker with ice add:
1 ounce of gin
1/2 ounce of lemon juice
2 dashes of simple syrup
4 ounces of champagne

Shake and strain into a champagne flute

Garnish with a lemon wheel

Between The Sheets
(Mr. Lee)

In a cocktail shaker with ice add:
1 ounce of cognac
1 ounce of light rum
1 ounce of triple sec
1/4 ounce of lemon juice

Shake and strain it into a chilled cocktail
glass

The Dirty Bastard

(The Groomsmen)

In a shaker with ice add:
2 ounces of Irish whisky
1 ounce of lime juice
1 ounce of ginger beer
1/2 ounce of ginger syrup

Shake and strain into two large shot glasses

The Cement Mixer
(Tim-The Bachelor Party)

This cocktail is not recommended for consumption.

In a shaker with ice add:
1 ounce of Baileys
1 ounce of lime juice

Shake and strain into a large shot glass

Gingerbread Cookie Cocktail
(Realtor's Christmas Party)

In a cocktail shaker with ice add:
1 ounce of vanilla vodka
1 ounce of Baileys Irish cream
1/2 ounce of Kahlúa coffee liqueur
1 ounce of gingerbread simple syrup

Shake and strain into a Christmas coffee
mug

Add a dollop of whipped cream

Sprinkle brown sugar on top

Santa's Helper
(Realtor's Christmas Party)

In a cocktail shaker with ice add:
2 ounces of spiced rum
4 ounces of eggnog

Drizzle caramel sauce onto the sides and
bottom of a martini glass

Shake and strain into the martini glass

Add a few mini marshmallows to float on
top

The Santa
(Realtor's Christmas Party)

In a blender with ice add:
1 cup of frozen strawberries
4 ounces of tequila
1 ounce of lime juice or triple sec
1/2 ounce of simple syrup

Rim the margarita glass first with corn
syrup, then with crushed red sugar

Pour the blended strawberry margarita into
the margarita glass

Garnish with a fresh strawberry

The Grinch
(Realtor's Christmas Party)

In a cocktail shaker with ice add:
2 ounces of vodka
1 ounce of Midori liqueur
1 ounce of pineapple juice
A splash of Sprite

Rim a large martini glass first with corn
syrup, then with crushed green sugar

Shake and pour into the martini glass

Shirley Temple
(Patrick)

In a cocktail shaker with ice add:
6 ounces of Sprite
1/2 ounce of grenadine

Shake and pour into a highball glass

Add maraschino cherries on top

Candy Cane Cocktail
(The Santa Wedding)

In a cocktail shaker with ice add:
2 ounces of strawberry vodka
4 dashes of white crème de menthe
2 1/2 ounces of cranberry juice

Rim a large martini glass with simple syrup,
then with crushed candy cane

Pour the mixture into the martini glass

Garnish with a mini candy cane

Sugar Cookie Martini
(Hotel Staff Christmas Party)

In a cocktail shaker with ice add:
1 ounce of vanilla vodka
1 ounce of amaretto
A splash of Baileys Irish cream
A splash of whole milk

Rim a large Martini glass first with vanilla
frosting, then dip in multi-colored sprinkles

Shake and strain into the martini glass

Garnish with a sugar cookie

**If you enjoyed this book,
you may enjoy other books by
Leah Orr:**

Murder at the Opulence Hotel:
The Executive Suite - Book 1
The Bartender - Book 2

Horror Shorts:
The Old Lady in the Gazebo
One Wish
The Last Mile
Till Death

Children's Books:
Messy Tessy
It Wasn't Me
Kyle's First Crush
Kyle's First Playdate

Coming Soon: The She Shed

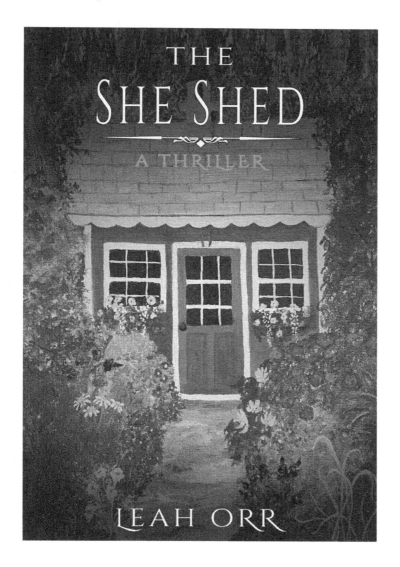

Special Thanks

I wish to thank my editor, Anna Roberts, for her editing expertise and finesse. I would also like to thank my mother for help with character development. A special thank you to former Officer Wendy Yanes-Alicot for her assistance with police procedure, norms, and etiquette, and Edward O'Donnell, criminal defense attorney, for his help understanding criminal protocols and procedures within the police department and court system. It has been a great pleasure to work with local comedians Casper McConnell and Jason White for their inspiration and authentic jokes enjoyed by old man Wilcox.

About the Author

Leah Orr worked in hospitality management. She lives in Jensen Beach, Florida with her husband and three children.

Leah donates the profits from her books to the Cystic Fibrosis Foundation to help find a cure for her youngest daughter and other children whom are afflicted.

Made in United States
Orlando, FL
28 January 2022